I NEVER TALK ABOUT IT

Véronique Côté
and Steve Gagnon

I NEVER TALK
ABOUT IT

Translated from the French by
37 different translators, one for each short story

QC FICTION

Revision: Peter McCambridge
Proofreading: Riteba McCallum, Elizabeth West, David Warriner
Book design and ebooks: Folio infographie
Cover & logo: Maison 1608 by Solisco
Fiction editor: Peter McCambridge

Copyright © 2012 by Les éditions du Septentrion
Originally published under the title *Chaque automne j'ai envie de mourir*

Translation Copyright © Baraka Books (QC Fiction imprint)

ISBN 978-1-77186-109-0 pbk; 978-1-77186-110-6 epub; 978-1-77186-111-3 pdf;
978-1-77186-112-0 mobi/pocket

Legal Deposit, 3rd quarter 2017
Bibliothèque et Archives nationales du Québec
Library and Archives Canada

Published by QC Fiction
6977, rue Lacroix
Montréal, Québec H4E 2V4
Telephone: 514 808-8504
QC@QCfiction.com
www.QCfiction.com

QC Fiction is an imprint of Baraka Books.

Printed and bound in Quebec

Trade Distribution & Returns
Canada and the United States
Independent Publishers Group
1-800-888-4741 (IPG1);
orders@ipgbook.com

Société
de développement
des entreprises
culturelles

Québec

We acknowledge the support from the Société de
développement des entreprises culturelles (SODEC) and
the Government of Quebec tax credit for book publishing
administered by SODEC.

Funded by the Government of Canada
Financé par le gouvernement du Canada | Canada

Contents

Introduction   9

1. Olives   15
2. Attic   20
3. Ants   25
4. Wrestling   30
5. Spasm   36
6. Detective   41
7. Tractor   47
8. Orange   53
9. Nightmares   59
10. Couch   65
11. Conspiracy   70
12. Modigliani   76
13. Cupcakes   82

14. Snot   88
15. Light   93
16. Sunglasses   98
17. Rice   103
18. Knives   108
19. Trolls   113
20. Dishes   119
21. Home   124
22. Ice   129
23. Looks   135
24. Notebook   140
25. Brothers   145
26. Rabbit   150
27. Cinema   155
28. Constellation   160
29. Flood   165
30. Pandas   170
31. Puberty   175
32. Missiles   180
33. Tsunami   188
34. Churches   193
35. Collection   198
36. Floorboards   204
37. Vinyl   213

About the Translators   219
About the Authors   229

Introduction

IT'S LIKE WHEN YOU'RE STANDING in front of a classroom of children. "Go ahead," you tell them, "there are no wrong answers." The next word out of their mouths is practically guaranteed to be a wrong answer.

So, in translation, we can't say there are no wrong answers, but there are few wrong answers. *J'ai 12 ans*. There's a difference in "wrongness" between "I am 13 years old," "I have 12 years old," and "I am 12 years." There's even a difference between "I'm 12" and "I am 12 years old."

QC Fiction was set up to do things differently and the idea behind this project is to get people thinking about the translators responsible for the words they're now magically reading in English. Not necessarily to give them recognition or a pat on the back. (Not all are deserving of a pat on the back.) But to acknowledge the process of translation, a reflection in a mirror or a puddle. What are their backgrounds and approaches? Have they twenty years' experience or have they never translated before? Are they award-winners or unpublished translation students? Does it matter?

This is, I think, an important conversation to have (and the rarity of such a conversation is partly alluded to in my choice of title: *I Never Talk About It*). Translations are the product of a set of translators with established routines and practices. With the same tics, favourite words, and go-tos as the rest of us. But none of this is ever discussed. Readers are lucky to find the translator's name on the book, let alone learn anything about their approach to it or the questions that kept them up at night.

In the occasional interview after the translation's release, the translator will say something like, "This is more an adaptation than a translation." Remember: there are few wrong answers. This isn't a sin or a failing, it is what it is. But wouldn't it be wonderful to have that on the book for all the world to see? "Freely translated by X," "Faithfully translated by X." (Best of all, wouldn't it be wonderful to have different translations of the same book? This happens in Russian literature, for example. But even there we need to do a little digging around a particular translator's reputation when deciding which translation to choose. Constance Garnett? Pevear and Volokhonsky? Marian Schwartz? Wouldn't it be truly great to have different translations of Nicolas Dickner or Elena Ferrante to choose from or switch back and forth between?)

Of course, the argument goes, "faithfully" would win the day. Because readers want to read faithful translations, don't they? Readers who are served a steady diet of faithful translations that cling to the original—translations that they seldom read let alone buy—are dying to read a faithful translation, aren't they? Well... what if they aren't? What if they're interested in a different sort of artistic creation? In a new work that's beautifully written in English and was inspired by words originally put down in French? Or in a version that lies somewhere in between?

What if? we thought. Let's give readers a choice. Let's start a conversation. Let's talk about the types of translators and translations you'll come across in this book. Let's show you a few of the possibilities. Let's have each of the 37 stories translated by a different translator. By a translator with his or her own unique approach. By a translator who then reveals a little of what they did and why at the end of each story.

None of which is to say that these are not successful translations; this is more than a translation exercise. They have been edited and polished, not simply printed. But they haven't been standardized or made to conform to some ideal. They have, of course, been read alongside the French. Probing questions have been posed. Second drafts have been sent. Liberties have been taken, and every word has been dutifully looked up in a dictionary. The authors have been asked exactly what they meant by such-and-such a word. In short, they are polished translations like any other published translation. They are just a little more upfront about the whole process. Because QC Fiction genuinely believes that if you read Eric Dupont in English there will always be a little of Peter McCambridge's or Sheila Fischman's voice in there. That Samuel

Archibald would sound different in English if he hadn't been translated by Donald Winkler. That this isn't an unavoidable failing; it just *is*.

Chaque automne j'ai envie de mourir seemed the perfect hybrid text to examine from a few different angles. Each short story came in fact from the theatre and was originally performed outdoors in Quebec City, with the audience literally wandering in off the street to a garden of secrets, then on to the next story somewhere else across town. (No surprise, then, that so many translators refer to the texts' oral nature or sometimes eccentric punctuation.) The monologues had been co-written by Véronique Côté and Steve Gagnon, with no indication whether a particular text had been written by one, the other, or both. Not counting the interventions from everyone else involved in the theatre festival, and then the editing process when the stories were first put together and published in book form.

It seemed exciting, and fitting, to have these stories translated by a broad range of people. By sleep-deprived young parents juggling newborn babies; by men and women, straight and gay; by people with French as their mother tongue; by people born speaking English who now only speak French and vice versa; by newbies and unpublished students and award-winning translators on speed-dial; by people who only speak enough French to order a croissant; by people who grew up speaking various forms of English in Ireland, England, the United States, and Australia; by retired French teachers; and by people who haven't picked up a book in years.

We hope it will be fun to read each of these stories. To compare them. To compare X's approach to Y's. To have each particular approach set out for all to see. And, most of all, the next time you pick up a book in translation, to wonder "What approach did this translator take?" Because there's always an approach, always a slant, always a distortion or deviation from the original, however slight or well-intentioned. Often it makes for a smoother reading experience in English. But it's nice to know it's there, all the same. To have something to think about. Because there are few wrong answers. Because any translation is a question and then an answer. A series of decisions that all lead to different places.

It's time to explore some of them.

Peter McCambridge
Fiction editor, QC Fiction

1. Olives

I NEVER TALK ABOUT IT. Not even with my boy-friend. Nor with my sister, my best friend, my mum. It's humiliating, totally. I don't want the people I love to notice, I don't know how I'd be able to go on afterwards.

No-one knows about it because I'm really, really good at making sure it doesn't show, at just seeming like it doesn't bother me, at letting stuff go, y'know. I don't understand people who aren't like me. At one point, I was even scared it was a kind of obsessive-compulsive thing, a sort of disorder, a problem in my head, a little knock, you know, but no. That's not it. I don't count how many walls there are in my bedroom fifty times before falling asleep, I don't freak out when I walk a number of steps which isn't a multiple of ten, I step on the cracks in the pavement, there's no routine I have to carry out before I leave my place, I don't do housework all the time. I'm normal, I think. As much as that means anything. No, it's, it's sneakier, more... hidden away.

It doesn't look like I'm counting. But I do. The exact tip. The length of the long-distance calls to my mum. The degrees on the thermo-stat. Films rented, days late, the cinema. How many loads from a bottle of washing liquid. How many bowls of cereal in a family-sized box. How many times I listen to a CD, if I finish a book or if it slips from my hands, and if so, how many pages I've read. Guests. How much shampoo they use, toothpaste, cleanser, hot water, beer, biscuits, olives, after-dinner drinks, coffee, toast, peanut butter. Toilet paper, for Christ's sake. I count bus tickets, how much time I've got left on the ticket to change buses, miles, petrol, parking. Transactions on my bank card. Drink bottles I paid deposits on. Electricity. That's great actually because it looks like I'm doing it for the planet, I don't hide that, I make out that I'm a greenie. To tell the truth, I think I am pretty green, it doesn't make any difference, having my reasons for being careful doesn't change anything. Anyway. It's not a mental illness, that's what I want to say. It's just... ugly. It's just sad. I know which of our friends have invited us to dinner, how many times, and who we've invited in turn, I remember who never brings a bottle of wine, and I even know who brings GOOD wine and who brings cheap stuff, I see it, I can't help it, I notice it and I count it, I can't do anything but. I know who I've bought drinks for and who's never bought me any. I know exactly how much I've earned every year since I finished high school. I know how much I've got in my pension schemes, I know how much I pay in bank fees, I know exactly how many days I could hold out for with what I've got at the moment, how long, using the insurance money, I could get by for if I was suddenly unable to work anymore.

I calculate everything. Always. That's just how my brain's built. It disturbs me. I can't accept a casual gift, I think of what I owe, of my new debt, as soon as someone tries to surprise me they mess me up completely, but it's not their fault, so I say nothing. Most of my energy in daily life is used up on hiding this part of me that's afraid of missing out on something. I don't know where it comes from. I envy people who can simply ignore it. There are people who don't worry, ever, that staggers me. There are people who have two hundred bucks in their account and that's it! They don't know when they'll be paid next, and that doesn't make them fall apart, I don't understand it, I'm totally jealous. I tell myself I'll never be able to go on a holiday unless it's all-inclusive. I tell myself I'll never be able to have a baby. I tell myself my parents should have taught me one thing in life, that nothing is missing. Like Buddha, or a monk, or a poem would say, nothing is missing, life has absolutely everything, everything is here, I mean: I've never wanted for anything, why, why am I so scared that all that might change?

I tell myself I'd like to just buy a dress for once on the spur of the moment, new shoes, perfume, walk along the pavement in spring and think about nothing but my boyfriend, who I'm off to meet up with at our friends' place, and have the glass of white wine that I'm handed when I get there without suffocating myself with anxiety. Nothing is missing. I know. I just can't get that into my head.

Tremblingly translated by Tony Malone

ABOUT THE TRANSLATOR

Tony Malone is an Anglo-Australian literary reviewer. His site, *Tony's Reading List*, has developed a strong focus on literary fiction in translation, featuring around one hundred reviews of translated literature every year. His reviews have also appeared at *Words Without Borders* and *Asymptote*. This is his first attempt at literary translation.

THE TRANSLATOR'S APPROACH

"After reading this story several times, I got a rough draft down on paper fairly quickly (with the help of several online sources for Quebec expressions!). However, I continued to work on my translation to make sure I had got a feel for the writer, making sure I didn't pitch the level too high for what was essentially a spoken text. Hopefully the voice that comes across in the English is similar to that of the original piece."

2. Attic

MY MOTHER WAS ONLY SEVENTEEN when I was born. She was studying to be a flight attendant. My father was older; he was twenty-four and already an airplane pilot. Since he was often away, we lived in an apartment above my grandparents, those on my father's side, so we could be near people we knew, people who'd come over to help my mother or babysit me, sometimes, when she went to work or out with friends. She worked her whole life "just for a short while, just in the meantime" for some sort of caterer who served meals at receptions. My mother hated her job. But I absolutely loved going to work with her, touching and tasting everything. I thought her little outfit very lovely, her small blue dress with a large white collar really attractive. And I'd tell her she was beautiful in her outfit, saying: "Mom, you look amazing in that outfit!"

But my mother hated her outfit, hated her job, and hated people talking about her outfit and her job.

Our apartment was under the roof, my grandfather called it the *attic*, and I know my mother got really pissed off whenever someone told her she lived in the attic, even if it wasn't really the case. Perhaps she frowned on my grandfather's jokes because she really felt as though she lived in an attic.

My mother had a small room, almost a closet, with a sloped ceiling, but with a huge window that took up most of the wall. I wasn't allowed in there. It had a rocking chair and a small cabinet where she placed the postcards my father sent her from all the places he travelled. She asked him to do this, to send her postcards from all over the world. My mother would sit in the chair and smoke cigarettes. I couldn't bother her, that was very clear, when she was in there smoking. When I had to ask her something, I remember sitting in front of the door, waiting for the smoke to stop before knocking.

Each time, I'd hear my mother sigh, her moment was over; she'd open the door and walk out quietly, her eyes often filled with tears.

I think becoming a stewardess was one of my mother's fondest dreams. I think she dreamed of going away with my father, seeing the world, always being somewhere else, and sleeping in hotel rooms. She likely would have tired of it someday, but since she never tried it, never did it, she grew very sad and disappointed. Her life wasn't what she wanted. She lived in an attic and suffocated from living there, from taking care of a child almost on her own, and serving bad coffee in pale green and pink reception halls. She'd never wanted this.

And I really felt it.

I felt it all the time, I was uncomfortable, I was always afraid of bothering someone. I never felt close to her. I thought she was beautiful, I wanted to be like her, I observed her, but my mother remained a stranger. She was like a movie star, an idol, someone you admire, look at from a distance, and sometimes approach with discomfort and embarrassment, heart pounding. I was nervous when speaking with my mother, as nervous as I'd have been speaking with Nathalie Simard.

I think there was even a sort of rivalry between us, as though she absolutely didn't want me to do great things, things I like, or fulfil my dreams. It could have been otherwise: she might have told me to avoid making the same mistake, encouraged me to never give up, to always carry on. But that wasn't the case; in fact, it was the opposite. As though my gain would have been her loss.

My mother died last year. Our relationship had always been strange. I got a postcard two weeks later; it was a photo of our old house, that of my grandparents, where we'd lived in the attic. She'd snapped a picture of our old house and made a postcard from it. On its back, she'd written: "Forgive me. Mom."

It's neither sad, nor kind, nor a nice gesture, nor a good way to go. It changes nothing about our relationship, my mother wasn't a better mother, it changes nothing about that. It doesn't mean "I love you," it doesn't mean any of this. All it means is "I'm sorry" and that's good, it's good that she apologized, so I'm more comfortable with this, because, for the first time, she also admitted that there'd been something

between us—rivalry, awkwardness, bad timing—
and she was apologizing for it. But it's a shame
my mother and I knew each other that way. That
our story ends with "I'm sorry." It isn't sad. It's
a shame.

Fluidly translated by Jean-Paul Murray

ABOUT THE TRANSLATOR
A writer and certified translator, Jean-Paul Murray
is secretary of the Gatineau Park Protection
Committee. The former managing editor and
English translation coordinator of *Cité libre*, he
has translated fifteen books, including novels
by Robert Lalonde and Louis Hamelin. Ekstasis
will publish his translation of Robert Lalonde's
Le monde sur le flanc de la truite in the coming
months.

THE TRANSLATOR'S APPROACH
"I tried to respect the author's voice while rendering the text into idiomatic English with as much
music as possible."

3. Ants

THERE WERE ANTS in the yard when I was young, on the concrete slabs at the bottom of the stairs. I loved them, and I hated them.

Sometimes they made it into the house and we had to chase them out because it drove my mum mad to find them there, forming a queue along the counter. She'd yell out that the house was made of wood and the ants, so I understood, would eat our house if they wanted to. I loved them outdoors, hated them indoors; and it was the same thing. I loved them and hated them in the same breath.

Outside, I let them crawl up my arms and enjoyed the little insect kisses that gave me goosebumps. The ants'd be here, forever; the summer'd be here, forever; I'd be loved, forever. Inside, I told on the ants to my elders and betters and left it to them to protect us, my home and me.

There'd be a home, forever, and I'd be inside, forever.

I followed the little creatures around with sticks; I gave them breadcrumbs; I put obstacles in their way and turned them around in every direction. I must have killed loads of them without ever realising.

But then one day I crushed one, hard, and after prodding it to see it get up, after seeing that that wasn't working, I asked my dad why it wasn't moving and when it was going to move again.

"She'll never move again 'cause she's dead."

That's what he said, and the idea that a thing can't ever come back again swept inside me like a great, cold wind. *Never.* The word entered my heart: *never* again, *never* again; and I suddenly understood. The body ends. Life ends. Summer, love, home, ants; they've all got an end. All creatures, one day, will never move again.

I've lost lots of things since. Two houses— my parents' one and one that caught fire. A dog I loved. My grandmother, Rose. My cousin

Philippe, who was twenty-one and taught me the names of birds, who played guitar and was afraid of girls, even though he was as beautiful as a wild horse.

I lost my dad. Never again: my dad. That, that took me a while to understand.

And other men too, men who didn't die but left. Who won't ever come back again.

I learnt early that things pass on. Then I had to face facts: love also passes on. Even the great loves, they pass on.

A much-loved daughter-in-law.

A lake.

Two friends.

All those scarves I really liked.

I also lost a few rings, about four or five, I'd say; some earrings too, including one pair I got as a gift, which I loved.

I lost a sleeping bag on the first day of my first trip to Europe. A camera that belonged to my mum. Dozens of photos.

The entire contents of a computer drowned in a glass of water.

I lost time. But with time, you never know, really, what's been lost and what's been gained.

I lost memories, too. Sometimes I did it on purpose, sometimes I buried the memories deep inside my head—I still have pictures of nameless European cities that appear to me in dreams, but they might get lost quickly, without any place names.

I've learnt to let those things that want to leave, leave; and to welcome those that want to come.

Things end. That's what makes them beautiful.

Stories end. That's what makes their beginnings make sense.

Countries, songs, hopes, gardens. Ants. People. One day, everything dies.

Now I love death and I hate death; the same thing in the same breath. I think of it every day. And it fills me with life.

Reasonably translated by Farrah Gillani

ABOUT THE TRANSLATOR
Farrah Gillani studied French at school in England, but has managed to avoid it ever since! She is, however, passionate about literature, studying English at Cambridge University and now running an online magazine in Luxembourg. In between, she

worked in marketing for Mars, where she was paid in both chocolate and money.

THE TRANSLATOR'S APPROACH
"My main concern in translating the piece was to ensure the language reflected the age, class, and personality of the protagonist. I decided to use simple words to provide her true voice whilst maintaining a starkness of tone that gives her story its beauty."

4. Wrestling

MY DAD is Hulk Hogan.

Well, truth is, my dad, he's more of a Super Mario type lawyer, but for years, after dinner when it was time to do the dishes, he was Hulk Hogan, and me, I was the little Karate Kid who would rather laugh than fight. My mom, she was the one who would stroke my hair and scratch my back when I got into her bed to sleep beside her, while they were watching TV. My dad, he was the one I fought with, every night around six thirty, just after dinner. We used to fight every day, while *Les détecteurs de mensonges* was playing in the background, until

I moved out of the house. Out of their house. At twenty-three.

We never wrestled after that.

It was a kind of ritual, to decide which one of us would do the dishes that night (and it was me more often than not, I mean, really more often than not, you know?).

It was a ritual of love, too. Yeah, of love.

Of deep affection, of tenderness filled with pride, and of great complicity.

There was, in our wrestling moves, an extraordinary passion that always came directly from the admiration we had for each other.

I admired the strength my father had inside him. Not just the physical strength, no. All his emotional strength, too. His strength of character. His self-assurance. His simplicity.

I think on his side he admired my lightness of mind, and the confidence I have that everything's gonna be all right. I'm still a pretty confident guy, even today, most of the time. I'm the confident type. I'm not naïve, though. And certainly not retarded.

As I get older, I look more and more like my dad.

Him and me, we're like two big silent teddy bears.

Silent, but not deaf and not without winks and not without arms and mouths to smile at each other with.

Underneath our professional wrestling suits, we have little jackets on, with pinned stars and silk bow ties around the neck.

Underneath the suits, we're like the human version of those stuffed animals they sell at The Bay over the holidays.

Those moments together, they didn't need words, those moments were better than words actually, because they were stronger than all the words put together. They were sincere, they couldn't be insincere because they were so totally spontaneous. Even when it became something that we did each day, it still kept that feeling of spontaneity. To find the strength, the energy, the adrenaline that was needed, it had to come directly from the heart. There's nothing like rage or being friends with another guy (well, that's just my two cents theory, but still), there's nothing like rage or being friends with a guy to put you in the mood for a fight. Both are connected to the heart. And us, it wasn't rage that drove us to punch and trip each other.

I never needed words to say that I loved him, and he never needed them either, we had other ways.

Nowadays, I don't live with my parents anymore. My dad and me, we don't wrestle anymore.

Now I do my own dishes, and he does his.

Now we each have our own remote control.

Now I don't hide anymore to eat his chips and his candy bars.

I hate wrestling, I never watch it on TV, and I certainly don't go to the cinema to watch the special events on the big screen.

But the wrestling that we did in the living room at my parents', the wrestling we used to do on the sofa, now that I really miss.

I feel a real longing for wrestling. For that particular kind of wrestling. I feel this need, this unfulfilled need, for a good fight.

Not out of rage.

Out of love.

Out of pride filled with tenderness.

Out of admiration.

I never talked about this with my dad. Probably because we never managed to develop a common language, we never got used to the fact that there were words between us.

I never talked about it with my dad, but at home, in my workspace downstairs, I keep a poster of Hulk Hogan, just above the wood workbench. And it remained a kind of inside joke, that. Hulk Hogan remained a kind of inside joke between him and me. And at Christmas, or on our birthdays, we still buy all kinds of crap for each other, silly things, calendars, cups, old mags, all kinds of stuff with his face on it, Hulk Hogan's face.

For some it's The Beatles, for some it's Elvis. For us, it's always Hulk!

It isn't exactly the same as getting slapped in the face, or feeling his strong hands pinning mine behind my back, but then again, it's kind of like we could still do without words to say what's really important. To say how much we hate each other's guts!

Muscularly translated by Daniel Grenier

ABOUT THE TRANSLATOR
Daniel Grenier was born in Brossard in 1980. In 2012, he published his first collection of short stories, *Malgré tout on rit à Saint-Henri* (Le Quartanier). As of today, he has translated

six books for different Quebec publishers like Marchand de feuilles, Boréal, and La Peuplade. In 2014, he completed a doctoral dissertation about the novelist character in American fiction from 1850 to 2007. His first novel, *L'année la plus longue* (Le Quartanier), was published in English by House of Anansi Press in March 2017.

THE TRANSLATOR'S APPROACH

"I've been translating professionally for three years now, but I've always translated in my head, as a reader, it's part of the fun. To translate in a language that is not your own is a destabilizing experience, it brings you back to the humbling feeling that's such an important part of the job. It makes you remember that the devil is in the details, and that to understand something is quite different from saying it, or even repeating it. Each time I try, and it's not often, I'm reminded of that simple fact: English, under the easygoing appearance it presents to the world, is so subtle, so difficult, it's as difficult and as hard as a diamond."

5. Spasm

SOMETIMES I FEEL THESE TREMORS inside that are pretty extreme under the circumstances.

They're like spasms, violent jolts, but I can control them, I totally can, I can draw them inside, squeeze them or I don't know, box them up, press them down, but still I get them, and I see how somebody might one day grab a baseball bat, a knife, or even a gun, leave the house, and go on the attack.

Bam!

Sometimes objects set me off. Sure, it's smarter for me to direct a spasm at something inanimate, but still. I fantasize about whacking my computer with a hammer or smashing all my dishes on the floor. Sometimes people set me off, and then I get scared. I want to hit them.

Hit them hard.

Bam! Bam! Bam!

Grab them by the back of the skull, grip tight, bash their forehead down on the table.

Once. Twice.

Three times.

Till they bleed.

Till their skull caves in.

I don't do it often. I don't do it ever. One of my problems is I look sixteen on days I'm all burned out and fourteen on days I'm rested and in good spirits, but inside, in my subconscious, something stops me from acting all innocent and smiley and childlike because with a baby face nobody takes you serious. Like when I go to Denny's with my folks and the waitress offers them a coffee and me a little glass of juice, it pisses me off, but because I'm a pissed-off guy with a baby face, nobody takes me serious, and because nobody takes me serious, it pisses me off even more. It's a huge endless vicious circle, and I constantly want to smack a waitress upside the head, burn down a 7-Eleven, smash up a Dunkin' Donuts, or clobber a dumbass bartender, or an overpaid civil servant who does jack shit all day, or a guy in India calling on behalf of Best Buy with his goddamn twenty-two-second delay every time we speak, or a rideshare driver who figures we're fated to become best buds, or a talk show host who cracks up at his own lame jokes, or some asshole I say I'm sorry to after I brush against him by accident and who then frigging scowls at me, or the three hundred and forty-seven other people a day I want to punch in the head or pummel till they're sorry they were ever born.

I don't know what'll happen if one day somebody gets all up in my face, I don't know what'll go down, but it terrifies me to think about it, to imagine that one day somebody might not chill before I do, because one thing's for sure, I'll never chill first. Never. I'll never chill. I'll never be okay with people being stupid, ignorant, hypocritical, spiteful, dishonest, I'll never be okay with people walking all over me, acting like jerks, being wasteful, looking down on me, tuning me out. I'm not the quiet type, and it's a good thing too because being quiet is basically being dead, but I'm a bit like a time bomb because if some dude stands in my way too long or laughs at me for losing my cool, I could attack, start totally hammering the guy, and even though I look small, even though I am small, I swear I might never stop. I can't ever get into a fight.

I'm the littlest kamikaze, the quietest, but I'm game, totally fucking game, and I'm ready, seriously fucking ready, to go head-to-head with the biggest sumo wrestlers on earth, they don't scare me with their big marshmallow bodies, their geisha hair, and their diapers for old geezers who piss themselves, but I'd rather not fight straight off, because it'd be brutal, man, a blood bath for sure, so instead I make my way slowly through the crowd, and sadly, in spite of myself, I absorb people's stupidities, I walk on alone, I absorb, I suck up everything in my path, and that's why I say I'm a little kamikaze because I'm the baddest, but I keep everything inside, I build a bomb inside me, and even though I'm not sure I'll use it one day, even though I'm not sure I'd even want to use it, I know it's there, that bomb of mine, that violence, that danger, I've got it inside me, and it's my strength, my awareness of the world around me, and it keeps me safe, I figure, from all the idiots out there, and it also stops me, I hope, from totally turning into an idiot myself one day.

Violently translated by Neil Smith

ABOUT THE TRANSLATOR

Neil Smith wrote the novel *Boo* (Hugh MacLennan Prize) and the story collection *Bang Crunch* (QWF First Book Prize). His fiction has been translated into eight languages. He was a finalist for a Governor General's Award for *The Goddess of Fireflies*, his translation of Geneviève Pettersen's debut novel.

THE TRANSLATOR'S APPROACH

"I translated this piece as though my target audience were Americans. As a result, I changed certain trademarks (for example, Tim Hortons became Dunkin' Donuts) and dropped a reference to Quebec TV host Éric Salvail (who became instead a lame talk show host)."

6. Detective

I HAVE ALWAYS THOUGHT I had big teeth.

I do have huge teeth. Gigantic teeth.

I hate my teeth no end.

My teeth are like giants living halfway out of my mouth. In the fresh air. Having an airing. Seeing the world at the same time as my eyes, or even before them. This is maybe why my eyes hate my teeth so much. The truth is I have two eyes and two teeth watching me at the same time, yet it's not the business of my teeth to be jutting out of my mouth and looking ahead.

I have always been ashamed of that.

It has always prevented me from smiling. It has always prevented me from laughing out loud. It turned me into a serious woman. Very generous, very open, very helpful, very loyal, yet somehow not very natural,

> simple

> or comfortable.

It turned me into a serious woman. An uncomfortable one.

I hold it against my teeth for causing all this mess.

I married a man with a huge nose.

A very curious, good-natured man, always eager to stick his big nose into everything.

A man of many habits who doesn't do anything that's not a habit already.

A man with a sensitive nose,

> as sensitive as his hands, his fingers and his eyes.

A highly meticulous man who does everything as a matter of habit, but always with great care, precision and thoroughness.

My husband has a huge nose and he puts it everywhere.

As a matter of fact, my husband is a private detective.

With his big nose, my husband makes a hell of a good private detective.

The alarm rings each morning.

At six thirty sharp.

Without exception.

And he always gets up. Carefully. Meticulously. Out of habit.

His curiosity will suddenly stick its big nose
out of bed, then with haste and curiosity and precision
my private detective will sink his big nose into his bowl of cereal.

He eats.

Although it's necessary to eat, I think that he wolfs down his cereal more out of habit than necessity. I hear him breathing from as far as the bedroom. The air goes in and out, unbearably, from his big, infinite nose.

Afterwards, he pushes his big nose into the shower first, followed by his little legs, little feet, then by his dwarf-like hands, his little mouth which never talks, and finally his childish, naïve head.

As for me, out of habit
in order to get through his own habits
I lie in bed until he is gone.

All day long, I have my huge teeth airing while my husband is poking his nose in everywhere.

I dry off my teeth in the kitchen, in front of the worktable

43

in the laundry room in front of the dryer

all over the carpets, the sweeper in my hand.

I spit out my teeth in the bathroom, on my knees, my head in the toilet bowl, my eyes popping out of my skull.

Then I dry my eyes. My mouth as well. I brush my teeth.

I dry my teeth in the bedroom, in front of our bed. Above the pillows that I put back into place.

I dry my teeth in the living room above the dusty TV set

in front of the clothesline

in front of the windowed-doors of the patio, in front of the mirror in our bedroom

and once again, in the bathroom, on my knees, my head in the toilet bowl.

Then I dry my eyes one more time. And my mouth. I brush my teeth. I lie on the floor for a while, my cheeks against the cold tiles.

I take a warm shower.

I dry my teeth at the IGA, pushing the cart with all my strength, my hands all clenched on the long handle, once in a while my feet on the metal bar. I let myself glide all over the place, quite fast. Nothing else helps my teeth dry off better than that.

When my husband's big nose is back home, it goes straight to my saucepans to sniff around.

My husband passionately recounts his day, the day of a curious private detective who has curiously looked for a place to stick in his curious big nose.

The day usually ends up early, as his big nose is exhausted from having been stuck into every garbage bin, every public toilet in hotels, hospitals, cinemas, dallying on the streets in the city, peeping through the windows of houses, garages, cars, barns, loitering all over the narrow lanes, airports, train stations, parking lots.

My husband never puts his big nose
>on my mouth,
>on my belly,
>to my ears to whisper a question,
>to my eyes to look for something beautiful, shady, or surprising or mysterious. A clue. A trace of something.

His big nose is never curious enough to come down between my legs
>or next to me on the pillow.

My husband is unwilling to put his nose into the depth of the wrinkles crisscrossing my face
>on my dried, worn hands

on my tired legs, getting older with every
new day.

He never tries to get me to show my big teeth,
never tries to make me smile.

That too turns me into a serious and uncomfortable woman.

Genuinely translated by Felicia Mihali

ABOUT THE TRANSLATOR

Originally from Romania, Felicia Mihali is a journalist, a novelist, and a teacher. She has studied
French, English, Chinese, and Dutch, and has specialized in postcolonial literature and history. She
now writes in French and in English.

THE TRANSLATOR'S APPROACH

"As a writer who never translates other than my
own texts, I ended up knowing a thing or two
about decoding somebody else's work. Here are
my new guidelines. 1) Read it until you know it by
heart. 2) Look in the dictionary more than you do
for your own books. 3) Don't be yourself. 4) Have
fun."

7. Tractor

I TOOK MY FIRST TRIP TO EUROPE five years ago. I was with my then-girlfriend; we started in Paris and followed almost the entire length of the coast, through Bordeaux, Biarritz and Arcachon until we reached the Pyrenees where we saw magnificent landscapes... haunted landscapes. Magnificent landscapes, but they were haunted and conspired against us.

We were camping and at first glance we looked pretty outdoorsy, but we were only camping because it was a whole lot cheaper, and it turned out to be more complicated than anything else and an even bigger pain in the ass since we had to schlep our tent around, and it was way too heavy, putting it up, taking it down, in short, we'll never do that again, but in any case, we were camping.

One morning we got up, we'd planned to climb the Pic du Midi de Bigorre, so we got up early, really psyched for it, and the tent got disgustingly hot in the morning anyway, so we left.

When we got there, we found out it was a fairly touristy place, but once we got further away, we discovered gorgeous scenery, it felt like we were in a movie, like we were in *Lord of the Rings* (minus the whole medieval thing). We were on sort of a hill with a really adorable river at the bottom of it. The greenery and the grass were beautiful, there were sheep off in the distance, everything was perfect. The only thing was that there was some kind of pony or whatever it was, but there was some kind of repulsive little horse and it had an erection and it kept walking around us. With an ERECTION! And another little detail, there was a big tractor doing who knows what, but it came to pick up some stuff not far from where we were, disappeared into the mountains and then came toward us to collect more stuff, disappeared again... like that, ad infinitum, like a ghost.

In fact, I think it was a ghost tractor that still haunts the Pyrenees to this day. But none of that kept us from lying down, my girlfriend and me, beside the river, from lying down more or less away from prying eyes, but in any case there weren't too many eyes around to see us and we were carried away by some sort of magic, lightheartedness, calm adrenaline; we were carried away by some crazy romanticism, we were deliciously detached from "whether or not this is suitable behaviour" and we made love. We TRIED to make love. This story happened in two parts. In the first, we kissed, touched each other, took off some of our clothes, I tried to penetrate her, the tractor arrived, I pulled out, we both lay on our backs, side by side, platonically, so that the tractor would think that nothing more was going on other than two lovers stretching out in the grass, the tractor went away, we started again, we kissed a bit, I tried again to penetrate her... this happened three or four times. That was the first part. In the second part, later, when I finally managed to stay inside her for a little longer, some kids, kids who came from I have absolutely no idea where, maybe they were children born of nature or the mountains, elves or angels, because I have no goddamn idea where

49

they came from, but kids most definitely showed up. We didn't know they were there at first, but we became aware of them pretty quickly since they were throwing rocks at us, rocks that were much too little to cause any sort of landslide—though they were still highly unpleasant when they landed on our faces and bums—so anyway, these kids came and threw rocks at us. I was in the Pyrenees with my girlfriend, I was magically penetrating her out in nature, it was good, there was a ghost tractor but we ignored it, and kids came and threw rocks at our asses and faces, I was in the Pyrenees, my shorts on the ground, half-erect and there I was, running through the grass. I ran through nature with my underpants around my ankles, running after those fucking little brats, and I heard them laugh, and at that precise moment, I swear, it was at that very moment that the pollen gave me an unbearable allergy attack, I was helpless as a newborn babe and just as naked, I was out of breath and butt-naked, I must have looked even more ridiculous than the pony with his erection, even more vulgar than the pony with his erection, and the pollen chose that very moment to give me shit, nature suddenly took on a whole new meaning for me, pulled the damn rug right out from under me. I turned back toward my girl-friend, who was traumatized, she wasn't angry or embarrassed, she didn't think it was particularly funny, she was completely traumatized, her happy-go-luckiness had taken a beating, I went back to my girlfriend, red as a beet, ah-chooing non-stop, we put our clothes back on, we left and returned to the tourist area, I had no desire to hike up the Pic du Midi de Bigorre but my girlfriend did, so we had a fight and finally went up in some kind of elevator, we felt ridiculous because it cost us 35 euros to go up the Pic du Midi de Bigorre in an ELEVATOR, and once we got to the top, we took about thirty pictures and then went back down.

For the past five years, I've had horrible allergies that start in May and only stop in September, I take Aerius every day, four months a year, I'm 22 and I've already taken 600 Aerius tablets in my lifetime and I hold the bratty little imps 100% responsible for this, I hold those kids wholly responsible for my allergies and also for the fact that sex with my girlfriend was never the same again. As if... I don't know. I don't know if you could call it a trauma, that's probably an overstatement, but I never again felt her completely let herself go when we made love.

Adeptly translated by Kathryn Gabinet-Kroo

ABOUT THE TRANSLATOR

American-born translator Kathryn Gabinet-Kroo has been a professional artist for almost 40 years, exhibiting her paintings in Canada and the U.S. Since completing her Master's in Translation Studies at Concordia University, she has been passionate about literary translation. Four of her translated novels have been published by Exile Editions, and excerpts have appeared in the Exile Quarterly and on the Ambos and Québec Reads websites.

THE TRANSLATOR'S APPROACH

"This quirky and colloquial text is full of run-on sentences so my translation had to accurately reflect its tone and stream-of-consciousness style."

8. Orange

EVERY SUMMER, you could say I have something like a crisis of faith, I feel down, I feel guilty. Every summer I get my act together and tell myself that I'm a grown-up, someone who's self-aware, like the ones I see every week at the market. I find it deeply ennobling to go there, I feel it's even more deeply ennobling to buy my fruits and vegetables from their stands and to go there all the time, to the market, hunting for fresh produce, grown here. I find it's a very inspiring place, in the end I find that food-radio personality Francis Reddy has a point: it's true that it makes us feel healthier, makes us feel closer to real life's truths. At the start of every summer, I tell myself that this will be good for me, going to the market, that it's right at the corner anyways, but finally, out of habit, I go only once or twice and that's it.

Except for this year.

It's only May, it's not even theoretically summer, but I've already gone a dozen times.

Because. Because there's a shop girl at the fruit kiosk by the entrance.

The fruit "toucher" at the entrance.

The shop girl whom I asked the other day, "Is orange season coming up soon?" And who answered me with a smile, "No, orange season is in the winter." I said, "Too bad." She replied, "Yes, it's too bad." And I said, eying those oranges that were just under her breasts, right before her navel, "Does that mean that these ones here are no good?" I could have said something else. I could have said something more intelligent instead of lobbing a dumb question posturing as an unfunny joke.

Being around her makes me want to eat all her fruit. The whole lot. I don't know if there's such a thing as eating too much fruit, but in any case, in my case, for the past month I've really been eating too much, I've been eating some every day and there are days when I throw some away because I stop by the market every two or three days and I haven't even come close to eating all the fruit I buy.

I don't know how to talk to girls. It was obvious before. Now it's crystal clear. All told, I'm pretty astonished by my inability to say anything intelligent or worthwhile to the pretty fruit vendor.

She looks like someone sculpted her from marzipan. I can't say that to her.

She looks like someone who smiles a lot and who's generally in a good mood most mornings. Maybe she even wakes up that way because she's been laughing in her dreams, maybe her waking up every morning is the result of an uncontrollable burst of dream-laughter. That's not something I can seriously ask her either. "Do you laugh in your sleep?" After a month of small talk about seasonal fruits, she finds me pretty strange.

I can't ask her if she has a boyfriend either. I don't get the impression that she does. In any case, I don't really care. I think if she does have a boyfriend, then she's not with the right guy.

I don't know where to begin. What's between, "Hello, how much are the tomatoes?" and "Hello,

I think you're beautiful. I think you're as beautiful as Île d'Orléans. I think your beauty is... as unbridled as a river flowing in springtime"?

I don't know what I could say to her.

And I'm pressuring myself more and more, because now she thinks I'm really into fruit. It's beginning to feel like there's no way out. And then, on top of that, another thing to keep in mind is that I'm worried she's beginning to think I'm gay because, realistically, even if it must be cute, it's not exactly virile for a twenty-five-year-old guy to stop in and talk raspberries and tomatoes almost every day, and to buy something every time under the pretext that I cook a lot, that I make the best turnovers, the best jams, the best tomato and parmesan tarts, that I can't wait for the small cucumbers to be in season so I can make my own dill pickles. None of which is true, for the record. I make no jam, I wouldn't know where to begin with jams, much less a tomato tart. I mean, dill pickles? Come on!

All told, what would've been much more virile would be to go, tomorrow, to see my lovely little gardener and to tell her, once and for all, that I've fallen for her, I think. But without the "I think" because that wouldn't sound too convincing and it would mute the overall desired effect. Is it possible to love someone in life if all they've ever done is smile and sell you fruit? Someone who just answers all your produce-related questions, who has only taken the time to laugh at every single one of your flat jokes, who has just chosen the best-looking strawberries for you? The answer is yes. I am proof that you can say whatever you want to someone for a disproportionate span of time, just so you don't have to say, "I love you." I am proof that we can jabber on endlessly about matters out of our reach just to keep from kissing the girl who gives you back your change. Being in love is overrated. When you think about it and you're not in love, it's not hard to feel like it will solve all your problems, that you'll at last find a way to live, a path to follow, that you'll have some control over your life and fate, that once you love, everything will make sense, fall into place, but no, it's more difficult than that. That's what Francis Reddy should talk about on his radio show, not all the different flavours of peppers. Because it doesn't help anyone to talk about peppers, about maple syrup or zucchinis or precocious strawberries. Fuck. Next time I go to the market, I won't buy any fruit, and I'll tell her I love her. I think.

Ambidextrously translated by Dimitri Nasrallah

ABOUT THE TRANSLATOR

Dimitri Nasrallah is the author of two award-winning novels, *Niko* (2011) and *Blackbodying* (2005). He is currently translating Eric Plamondon's 1984 trilogy and serves as editor for Véhicule Press's Esplanade Books fiction imprint. His third novel will be published in 2018. He lives in Montreal and teaches at Concordia University.

THE TRANSLATOR'S APPROACH

"For 'Oranges,' my first challenge was to get a sense of the narrator from the chapter without reading the rest of the book. I determined that to be 'rueful slang,' which is probably meaningless to others, but to my mind the term offered a template. With a notion of voice and temperament in mind, I set about trying to recreate the poetic intimacy of the first-person confession using what I considered to be the English parallel of 'rueful slang.' I was more interested in how the protagonist's Anglo cousin would play the scene than trying to accurately annotate the French. Hence the ambidextrous nature of the translation: two hands at work, one French, the other English. Again, most likely meaningless to others but useful to my working process."

9. Nightmares

SOMEWHERE IN DEEPEST EGYPT there's a pyramid inhabited by my father.

A white pyramid.

When my father was six he'd wake up in the middle of the night. Two a.m., three a.m.: that's when his father would come home, shit-faced, and he'd get him something to eat. He'd fry up eggs to keep his dad from waking up his mother. So they wouldn't fight.

My dad left school in Grade Seven, when his father died. He didn't get to be a lawyer when he grew up. He didn't get to be a pilot.

Things were always complicated between us. There was a lot of love, no shortage of love, but something else as well, a feeling of inferiority he always harboured. I think because, from a very early age, I was highly articulate and unshakeable in my convictions.

And also because I did so many different things. I did whatever I wanted. When I really wanted to do something I stuck it out and followed through.

I think he was scared I'd think he was a nobody, good-for-nothing, stupid, I don't know exactly—but something came between us, short-circuiting our connection. I guess when you get right down to it that's what it was, he felt somehow inferior. It was always there in our conversations, below the surface, waiting to bubble up. I'd be talking and suddenly he'd feel attacked.

I never thought my dad was stupid. The opposite is true: We're equally intelligent; we both share the very same, very keen intellect. Today my father moves me. I find him endlessly moving.

He could have accomplished great things. He would have so loved to accomplish great things. But he never got the chance, and that made him bitter. It's all too sad for words.

Today there's a pyramid in deepest Egypt that my father inhabits. Inside his hands have made their mark on walls of sand, and his voice is as quiet as a whisper in church.

But until I turned thirty my father inhabited my nightmares. Bizarre ones. He'd come to me in the night, get in my head. The setting was his old family home, the home I imagined him growing up in. He would be sitting down, I could see him from behind, his bent head resting in his hands. He'd go there and sit down and I would go there too, every time, and with an ominous sense of dread I would explore his house, his objects strewn over the floor like castoffs... As I walked toward my father I could hear him crying. It was a quiet, hollow sound, and it went on for hours, while I stood behind my father, in our dusty home, listening to him cry. It would go on well into the night, and I'd wake up in a state of total anguish; those dreams were unbearable.

Because I was having the dreams more and more often, and it was turning into an obsession—to the point where I was going to bed in fear of having the dream again—I eventually figured out what it all meant. You didn't have to be Sigmund Freud. I missed my dad. My dad was unhappy, had been unhappy his whole life, had never been able to do what he loved and there was nothing I could do about it, but I wasn't standing by him, wasn't there for him, and it was gnawing away at me.

Because I knew it had always been one of his greatest dreams, because he'd told me about it lots of times, and because he sure as hell wasn't going to make it happen on his own, I got up one morning and called him and said, "Get dressed, we're going to Egypt for two weeks." And that's just what we did. I meant it when I said "Get dressed, we're leaving": I meant exactly what I said because in the time it took him to get dressed and pack his bags I got in my car and drove up to the Saguenay to pick him up, and then we headed off to Montreal to catch our flight for Cairo.

My mom had no idea when we left. She was happy for us, she was really happy for my father and I, to see us head off together, and it's true it was a beautiful thing. She didn't know it at the time but she would never see my father again. And she loved him. She smiled; this was grand. She was happy for him, proud of him, so proud, as she saw him for the last time.

My father died in Egypt, in a white pyramid.

My father died in Egypt, overwhelmed that he'd finally made it.

His hair was full of sand, and so were his eyebrows, and he always had a few grains in his hands as well, it's true, he was constantly picking handfuls off the ground so he'd never be without sand in his hands. And Bach was playing in his head. There's no doubt in my mind. My father may not have been aware but as far as I'm concerned Bach was playing in his head, because Bach makes me cry and so does this story, the story of my father who died in a pyramid in Egypt. The story of my father who never believed in God, never believed in churches, never whispered in church because they didn't mean a thing to him, and then, all of a sudden, got down on his knees and turned to me, with his hand on his heart, and asked me to leave him alone.

I left quietly, and that was that. Turns out the Bach was in my head, not his.

Carefully translated by Pablo Strauss

ABOUT THE TRANSLATOR
Pablo Strauss grew up in British Columbia and lives in Quebec City. He has translated books by Daniel Grenier (*The Longest Year*) and Maxime Raymond Bock (*Baloney*, *Atavisms*), and short works by a variety of Quebec authors.

THE TRANSLATOR'S APPROACH

"Translating for me is a slow, unscientific process of writing and rewriting until you can't look at the piece any more. Experience has taught me that translation has no rules; the translations I love are at once loose and careful."

10. Couch

THERE ARE SO MANY good reasons why.

I have like these mini crises of... of anxiety, I guess. I don't want to call them panic attacks because that only makes me panic more.

I don't like the city. When I think of everyone who lives here all alone, I fall to pieces, come undone, can't go on.

Sometimes I cry about nothing at all and am afraid I'll never stop, never be able to work again or, worse yet, be able to leave my house again. Sometimes it just comes over me when I'm out on the street or at the grocery store.

There's this certain age in boys I find upsetting, just before adolescence, around twelve-thirteen years old. I see a boy that age all alone on a bus or eating quietly at some fast food restaurant, or about to rock out at a concert, and my heart splits. I don't know why.

Sometimes I break dishes all week long; not on purpose, just because everything slips out of my hands.

Whenever people tell me about illnesses or symptoms or tumours or STDs, I really don't feel well. It's as if some big viscous beast churns in my belly, and I realize for the first time it's inside of me, a kind of fat, slumbering snake that could start to writhe at any minute.

Whenever I see the ocean on holidays, I feel as if I've betrayed the best part of myself: I can't understand why I live so far from the ocean.

I've been so heartbroken that I vomited for three weeks straight.

I have this super intense sense of time passing. I remember when I was six, I was walking down my street, and I was thinking, "I'm six years old. Soon, I'll never be able to say that again."

I can't drive stick; it's like I've got this big, huge mental block. Who cares, but it's true. Total angst. Hyperventilation-style.

66

I can only fall in love if the guy's already in a relationship, living in another country or depressed.

Incidentally, I've been single for eight years now. At my age, seriously, that's just weird.

I don't even know what my wildest dream is anymore. That's really... I mean, that's bad.

I'm probably a hypochondriac.

Sometimes I'm afraid I might actually be nuts. Sometimes I'm afraid I'm just a pain in the ass.

Sometimes I'm afraid I'll only ever be happy when travelling.

In any event, I'm inconsolable—I don't know about what. That said, I suspect everyone is. Inconsolable.

There's this place inside of me no one can reach. It's a sort of island, or a cliff, impregnable, and that sometimes hurts so bad—physically, I mean—that I need someone to find that pain and suppress it with all their might so I can stop feeling it all the time. It's like a wound. Or a hunger. It's like a kind of love that I've had to stuff down inside, that had become like superheated metal.

I also know that even if I'm loved, I'll feel compelled to keep this to myself, this thing that pulses all the time. That glows red inside.

Sometimes I tell myself I could be less miserable.

Sometimes I tell myself that, I don't know, I could live a better life? Just take it easy. Sometimes I think about all of that, and it's as if... what? It could be less awful. I could feel less alone. Life isn't supposed to hurt all the time. That I know for sure.

But I can't go to a psychologist because...

Because I'm afraid I'll find out who I really am. And be even more miserable.

Yeah, that's it.

Intuitively translated by Lisa Carter

ABOUT THE TRANSLATOR

Lisa Carter is an acclaimed Spanish-to-English translator whose work has won the Alicia Gordon Award for Word Artistry in Translation and been nominated for the International DUBLIN Literary Award. Through her company, Intralingo Inc., Lisa helps authors and translators bring their works to a whole new audience.

THE TRANSLATOR'S APPROACH

"Since French is a (distant) third language for me, I decided to approach this translation as intuitively as possible. I didn't want to get caught up in dictionaries, puzzle through grammar and vocabulary, and in so doing lose the sense of the story and the sound of the words. I spoke each line aloud and then tried to repeat that in an English that felt as if it matched the original. Only after that first draft did I check whether I had misinterpreted any vocabulary or verb tenses, and fix whatever I had gotten wrong. For the next few drafts, I again relied on my ear to polish the English."

11. Conspiracy

SO, WHAT I'M GOING TO TELL YOU'S not very nice.
It's not great. I know. It's not... Actually I don't
think you're supposed to talk about this stuff.
So I don't. I don't talk about it. But I do think
about it.

I'd really like to carry on believing that the
world's not against me, that it's not picking on
me personally, it's just that things are getting
tough, seriously. I mean, at one point, it was like
WOAH! Like there's this massive conspiracy
to make me feel like a loser, all alone, no life,
no ambition, no partner, no love, no hope, no
plan, no one I even fancy other than celebs—

yeah, in my dreams—no... future, you know what I mean?

I'm not a bad person, I'm really not. I'm even pretty chilled. I've seen an insane number of films, I'm ace at Guitar Hero, I work my arse off and I really love my job. I've got a wicked sense of humour, I blog, I've travelled, I support Arsenal, I read the paper and I'm educated, so I can talk the talk. I'm up for a night out dancing, mooching round the shops, flat-sharing, partying... I can do anything—I read, I cook, I know loads of stuff... I'm super handy, I can light a barbecue or milk a cow, I make perfect mojitos, I'm almost veggie. When it comes to pop culture I'm a mine of information *and* I have a social conscience (they're not incompatible). I recycle, I buy Fairtrade and organic when I can, second-hand the rest of the time. I haven't got a car, I love life. Yeah, I love life. I'm super alive. I'm a winner. I'm funny, I'm nice. Except that I've really had it up to here.

I like kids, that's not the thing, I like kids, I'm brilliant with kids, and kids like me, but that's not the thing. It's just that, suddenly, out of the blue, a million pregnant women have just erupted all over the place. It's great, that's not the thing, I'm fine with life in general, but this! It's never-ending! It's too much!

I've had it up to here with babies, OK? Everyone's pregnant, there's kids running around all over the place, babies crying and mums who talk about nothing but their kids all day long. I don't want to take it personally, I don't want to start seeing it as an attack on me, but seriously, I'm close.

The other day I went to a baby shower and it was too much. The shower was just too much. Like, so surreal. It was all pregnant women and young mums. NO ONE else. All around me. I mean, it felt like a bad joke to wind me up—as if I was on *Candid Camera* or something. I think that out of like twenty women in their thirties, there were five of us who weren't pregnant and I'm not even exaggerating, not even if I wanted to. Even if I was allowed to.

Somehow, I found myself all on my own hemmed in by pregnant women. I was the only one drinking wine and I felt like getting pissed like some scumbag, but I didn't, 'cause I'm too nice for that. During the gift unwrapping, I was nearly suffocated by all the talk about babies–nappies–maternity-leave–cervical-effacement–cervix-5-centimetres-dilated–milk-flow–sleeping-through-the-night–activity-mats–baby-carriers–breastmilk–wee-poo–haemorrhoids-farts.

I nearly drowned, I looked all around like a hunted animal, desperately seeking a way out, an emergency exit, something, but instead of puking or passing out, I turned to my lovely friends and said: "Hey! How's about we talk about fucking up the ass?" And my amazing friends, who are nearly all pregnant too, my friends are so amazing, my pregnant friends are so fucking great that they got totally into it.

I talked about fucking up the arse with my pregnant friends in the middle of a baby shower, and I am so, so proud.

Well, proud's not really the right word. But at least we had a proper laugh.

Me, I'm not expecting a baby. Me, I'm waiting for something to happen—a snog, a love affair, even a shag, a fight, a hold-up, I'm waiting for a comet, a tornado, a tsunami... something. I'm waiting for all that but nothing ever happens to me.

The whole world's pregnant. I'd like to be happy for the whole world, but I'm just fed up.

(ir)reverently translated by Ros Schwartz

ABOUT THE TRANSLATOR
Ros Schwartz is an award-winning literary translator from French. Since 1979, she has translated over 70 works of Francophone fiction and
non-fiction including a new translation of *The
Little Prince* by Antoine de Saint-Exupéry and
nine works by Georges Simenon. Other authors
include Tahar ben Jelloun, Dominique Eddé, Aziz
Chouaki, and Dominique Manotti, whose *Lorraine
Connection* won a Silver Dagger Award. Founder
and co-director of the literary translation summer school at City University in London, Ros frequently leads workshops, is a regular speaker on
the international circuit, and publishes articles on
translation issues.

A Fellow of the Institute of Translation and
Interpreting and active member of the Translators'
Association of the Society of Authors, in 2009 Ros
was made a *Chevalier de l'Ordre des Arts et des
Lettres*.

THE TRANSLATOR'S APPROACH
"The key decision was whether to domesticate
the translation or not. Although there is a certain
amount of Québécois slang, the only two details
that firmly root the text geographically are 'je
prends pour le Canadien' (I support the Habs)
and a reference to the TV show *'Surprise sur prise'*.

But location is secondary to the character of the narrator and the central issue is the loneliness of the twenty-something whose friends are all in relationships and having babies, and her act of rebellion. A situation that is universal. And so I decided to transpose the setting to London and to substitute an English soccer team for Habs and an equivalent English TV show for *Surprise sur prise*.

I have a daughter of twenty-six, and it was her voice and the voices of her friends that I heard in my head throughout the monologue. I asked my daughter Chloe and her 'girls' to read the translation and give me feedback—which was crucial in pinning down the voice and vocabulary. Chloe and I had a session where she read the translation out loud to me and vice-versa, and I made further adjustments. I also drew on the recent British TV series *Fleabag* which features a woman in her late twenties/early thirties whose life is chaotic and who sets out to shock.

Finally, I read the translation out loud and recorded it, then adjusted the punctuation to reflect the natural speech inflections in English. My aim was to retain the spirit of the original but not the letter."

12. Modigliani

I FANTASIZE ABOUT MODIGLIANI'S PAINTINGS of nude women much more than all the porn on the whole Internet.

Because they smell like sex, real sex, good sex, the kind of sex that smells like sex, the kind with sweat, awkward hands, rough hands.

Because they smell like the 19th century, smell like alcohol, orgies, then the wretchedness of living.

Because the women in his paintings have exquisite breasts and that's why he wanted to paint them, because their breasts are exquisite. And probably their eyes, too, which I think are also exquisite, and sad.

I dream of painting a woman and then alternating between painting and sex. Let's pop some bottles, I'll paint a little, we'll make love, I'll paint a little, we'll make love.

I dream that it'd be in a dingy little hotel room in the middle of Spain or France, or in my ugly, totally undecorated apartment on a seedy street in Paris, but that it'd smell like sex all day and all night, in the floorboards, in the walls, and especially on my fingers.

I dream that we'd be surrounded by empty bottles, hundreds of cigarette butts, ash, dirty dishes, and empty frozen dinner boxes.

I dream of penetrating, without any protection, or modesty, or embarrassment, or thought of being tender or delicate, all the women's bodies that entice me.

I dream of penetrating all the women's bodies that entice me, in all the locations that entice me, without worrying about other people, general hygiene, adequate space, about "whose is this." Without worrying about if it's in the afternoon or at night, if we're in sight or not.

I dream of penetrating the woman leaning against a pole in the parking lot. In a gravel pit. In a dirty alley. In a cheap old motel room, with three women. In the middle of the living room at a party. In hundreds of bar bathrooms. With five different women, in the same bar, on the same night. I dream that they'd all take turns giving me blowjobs, in public restrooms.

I dream that I'd have as much as I want, whenever, with whomever. That it'd be quick, but good, that we'd be animals, perverted, unrestrained. That we'd only be doing it, fucking, forever, that we wouldn't think about anything except fucking, completely wasted.

I dream of always being completely wasted, always holding a bottle of wine, smoking hundreds of cigarettes an hour, taking every drug on earth in one night, being high for three days, taking a week to recover then starting all over again.

I dream of not giving a damn about other people's love most of the time, then sometimes wanting to burst with love for just one woman. Of hounding her, endlessly running after her, only thinking about her all the time, writing her long, violent letters where I'd speak of betrayal, suicide, and revenge.

I dream of being Modigliani.

I dream of being Musset. Feydeau.

I dream of being Baudelaire. Rimbaud.

I dream of living in the 19th century, going to brothels, completely drunk, taking a girl into the corner, pulling off my suspenders, pulling up my shirt, putting my hands on her breasts and making love to her, her and all the rest, until syphilis gets me.

I dream of making love to all those girls and painting them afterward. Painting them on huge canvasses, flinging brushstrokes wherever I want, without worrying about it, because that's what makes masterpieces pulsate with life, hunger, lust, desire, that's what appears from those strokes. I wouldn't hold anything back, I'd let it all explode onto the canvas. Let the women in my paintings all have the same face, a melancholic face, and let my colors always be the same, the colors of blood, sex, and then the beauty of living loose.

I dream of living loose. Of dying, completely wasted, after a couple years of orgies.

I dream of going back to a time when artists painted and wrote with urgency, with fervor, with passion, totally invested in themselves, in all their flesh, in all their hands, because they knew their lives would be brief and ephemeral, so their paintings and writings would be all that remained of them, and they would last a long time.

I dream of only needing to know a woman for a few minutes to be able to paint her exquisitely. I dream of having the balls to ask her to show me her cunt, and she'd agree to give it to me because within it, probably subconsciously, all our sadness and inadequacies erupt, but by some magic or invisible rule, we also give each other all our colors, our life, our intensity, in one fell swoop.

I dream of being young and reckless, living like that, hurting people around me maybe, but there'd be something in my every movement, something intense, pushing back against the norm, against unbearable waiting, pushing back against resignation, withdrawal, old-fashionedness. Pushing back against art that's too calculated and doesn't mean anything anymore.

Dying young, but my cock full of fucks and sex.

Unprudishly translated by Allison M. Charette

ABOUT THE TRANSLATOR

Allison M. Charette founded the Emerging Literary Translators' Network in America. She has received a PEN/Heim Translation Fund Grant and been nominated for the Best of the Net. Her translation of Naivo's *Beyond the Rice Fields*, the first novel from Madagascar to appear in English, is available from Restless Books.

13. Cupcakes

I HAVE A FRIEND I went to school with whose mother cooks like a chef. Not a word of a lie, she's unbelievable. She would blow everyone out of the water on *Top Chef*. Everything she makes is delicious—she's got the touch. So this friend and his mother have a sugar shack, and we've gotten into the tasty habit of spending the day there once a year, a day when his mother rolls out the red carpet, and we eat for hours non-stop, a mouth-watering, sugar-filled day, and we leave with our stomachs full, and, sometimes, feeling a bit like throwing up because we ate too much.

So my friend lost one of his sisters last November, just before winter. One of his sisters, the youngest one, killed herself. It was tragic because there's only one way those sorts of things can go. I saw the family fall apart, from pretty close up. I saw them not knowing what they were supposed to be doing with themselves anymore. I saw them trying to find their place, because the whole structure had just blown apart. I saw the mother, who had always been at home, lose sight of why she should be there, because there was no one in the house anymore, because the house was empty. I imagined the mother feeling betrayed, trying to find a reason, because someone had just killed herself in the basement of her house, the house she had always kept clean, more out of love than obsession, to make it nice, so people would feel good there, so they would feel good in her home. That mother had just figured out that feeling good isn't about floors and dust and Hertel at all. That it's something beyond our control, that it's not at all about chocolate cake, meatloaf and baked beans. It's as if all of a sudden, all of that sunk in. I think it must have been hard for her to realize that, to realize that even though her cakes were good and took us back to our childhood, even though her soup was hot and soothing, even though it was always great eating at her house, there are things that all of her will and all of her talent as a mother couldn't do anything about. And I think that, that feeling, that realization, I think it's hard to take, particularly like that. It rips you open and you just never close up again.

Last night, I saw my friend. We had a great time. I was happy to see him doing so well. We talked about everything except his sister. All night I wanted to ask how his parents were doing, how his mom was. In the end, I didn't talk about it because I was afraid that he wouldn't want to answer, and anyway, that wasn't the vibe at all. At the end of the night, I went to get my bag out of his car. He opened the trunk and said: "My mom made maple cupcakes. Want one?" There was a big Tupperware thing in the trunk with around ten perfect cupcakes inside, with icing and everything. I couldn't believe it. I was so happy because I love cupcakes, and because I think his mother's are the best. I took one, and I paused, and then we laughed and I took another.

They were disgusting. First I smelled them, and I didn't think they smelled like anything. I thought the icing was maple, that was the colour, like maple icing, and I tasted it, but no, it was like nothing icing. I would even go so far as to say it was more like Fleecy icing than maple, or whatever other soapy taste. I took a bite of the cupcake. It was disgusting. It was as though she had tipped the entire box of salt in it. The whole cupcake tasted like old flour. I almost spit out the first bite.

I still ate both cupcakes. I shoved them down one bite after another. I wanted to cry they tasted so bad, but I ate them both. I swallowed, I ate them without stopping, in one shot. It was a ritual. It was to honour her. It was a gesture of compassion, a silent scream. It was as though last night, I was eating, I was swallowing a bit of the woman who still gets up every morning. Still, and in spite of it all. Who is living, who is putting one foot in front of the other, who is distracted, who is no longer in the frame of mind for it, but who is still making cupcakes, because that's what she does best. She keeps making cupcakes like back when she was sure of herself, sure of her strength, sure of her power, convinced that her cupcakes would protect her kids, that that's part of what it takes to be a good mother, making the best cupcakes. I ate her disgusting cupcakes because she is carrying on and that's good to see, that she's still making them, but that now she doesn't give a shit whether they're good or not. She doesn't give a shit whether the flour tastes like the pantry or not. She couldn't care less if she adds too much salt. She couldn't care less that she didn't put any maple syrup in her maple cupcake icing. I decided to eat both cupcakes, not to throw them in the garbage, because I wanted to swallow a bit of her, out of compassion. I wanted to swallow some of the wrinkles that have cropped up like weeds on her face since November. Swallow a bit of her anger, her confusion, her fear, her sadness. I ate the cupcakes then I said to myself: "If she cried into them, if she blew her nose in them, I'd be happy," as long as she actually did it, as long as she had a really good cry in them, mixed the cake batter with her hands, punching it, as long as a bit of her rage, a bit of her feeling of abandonment, a bit of her feeling like she's not as good a mother are inside it, as long as that's all there and that's what I swallow, what I eat. It made me feel good to eat her cupcakes of death, her zombie cupcakes, her vacant stare cupcakes. It made me feel good to eat her cupcakes, and it was okay that they were no good.

Frantically translated by Rhonda Mullins

ABOUT THE TRANSLATOR

Rhonda Mullins is a writer and translator living in Montreal. She won the 2015 Governor General's Literary Award for Translation for Jocelyne Saucier's *Twenty-One Cardinals. And the Birds Rained Down,* her translation of Saucier's *Il pleuvait des oiseaux,* was a CBC Canada Reads Selection for 2015. She is also a four-time finalist for the Governor General's Literary Award in Translation.

THE TRANSLATOR'S APPROACH

"I had to listen closely to the voice in this short story, because it is unusual. So I repeated sentences over and over out loud until they sounded right(ish)."

14. Snot

I EAT MY SNOT. Because—well, just because. Because it's salty. And I like that. Salty things. Because I like the texture. Because it's free and I like free stuff. Because I'm high-strung and it channels my stress. Because I kinda like having a bit on my fingers.

Because I can't help it. When I feel a booger inside my nose, I can't think about anything else.

Because yeah, okay, you might call it a mental illness, but that's just how it is and anyway it's not that big of a deal.

Because in any case, there are worse things out there. I mean—there are people who rape children because they can't help it.

My thing doesn't hurt anyone.

Because it's natural. Every other animal does it and it doesn't hurt them.

Because, and I'd be willing to spend hours arguing this point, I'm convinced it's full of vitamins.

Because if it isn't full of vitamins, it must at least be full of minerals.

Because my body is my body and I'm not grossed out by it. (I might not go so far as to eat my turds, but whatever. That's not the same thing anyways.)

I'd never eat someone else's snot, though.

Because it doesn't make you gain a single pound. I may eat my snot but there are people out there who have seriously fat asses. I'd rather eat my snot than be obese.

Because I'm sure that 76% of the population does it but won't admit it.

Because it doesn't make me any more of a chump than the 1.5 million people in the world who watch *Deal or no Deal*.

Because in my opinion it's damn fine proof that we live in a free country.

Because some people scarf down speed, sperm, scotch, McDonald's, or kiss their cats, dogs, or ferrets on the mouth.

Damnit, because I see people in public washrooms who shit and then leave without washing their hands.

I eat my snot unconsciously, it's a vice, I know, and I could make an effort to correct it, but then I tell myself that if some people have such an anger problem they beat their wives or children and if some people are so cheap they slip sandwiches into their purses at a season opening at the Trident theatre, if some people are such liars they make everyone believe for thirty years that they've written a book and it's coming out soon, if some people are so selfish they let their parents die in old age homes, and if there are so many alcoholics, compulsive gamblers and junkie prostitutes who wreck their own lives and the lives of others, then I don't see why I'm the one who has to worry about the fact that I eat my snot! Yeah, ok, I eat my snot, but for fuck's sake I'm not the only one who should have to make an effort to be civilized and try and seem like I'm sane and well-adjusted. I'm not the only one who should have to make an effort to seem normal. Christ. We're up to our ears in mental cases who don't have a clue how to live and *I'm* the one who gets stared at when I eat my snot.

I may eat my snot, but at least I'm not in the army.

I don't have a big-ass truck spewing pollution just for fun.

I don't have kids by accident.

I don't give other people AIDS just because I don't give a shit.

I don't drive drunk.

I don't tell everyone to fuck off when I'm drunk.

I don't knife anyone in the doorway of the bar.

I don't do illegal deals.

I never put pills into anyone's glass of beer.

All I do is sit sometimes on a park bench or at home quietly in front of the TV—I just sit down quietly now and then and eat my snot.

Fuck!

Seriously. Does that really *bother* anyone?!

Gingerly translated by Jessica Moore

ABOUT THE TRANSLATOR

Jessica Moore is an author and translator. *Mend the Living*, Jessica's translation of the moving and unusual story of a heart transplant by French

author Maylis de Kerangal, was nominated
for the 2016 Man Booker International Prize.
www.jessicamoore.ca

THE TRANSLATOR'S APPROACH
"My approach to translating this story was loose,
but solid, like the Québécois pronunciation of
'j'aime ben,' and somewhat at arm's length."

15. Light

AT FIRST, IT WAS EASY. I could do it sitting down.
I could do it all the time, even at night, for he
slept in our room. Deep down, I suppose, I did
it out of fear, but the strange thing was that
I always finished up having a sense of peace seeing him like that, watching him breathing, doing
nothing but that, sleeping and gently breathing. Watching him doing it, making sure he was
doing it, ended up making me too breathe more
easily. There are so many stories of children who
stop suddenly, in the night, for no reason, for
nothing. That must be a nightmare, I would say
to myself, your child stopping breathing. It must

be hell, you must be plunged into hell if your baby stops. And you must wonder ever after why he stopped. Why you weren't there. Where you were when your child needed you to remind him to breathe. But mine breathed. Always. As if abandoned, in the best sense of the word, in the sense of trust and serenity, of 'I understand' or 'That's all I want.' At first, it was easy. It was only his breathing I had to keep an eye on. I took it on, I got very good at it, I was the guardian of his mouth, his breathing, his baby breath with its scent of milk and clouds. You have no idea the way life is turned upside down when a baby arrives. You don't know, you can't know, you can't imagine how much you are going to worry, always, all the time, every day, every night. You can't know in advance how fearful you will be watching him growing up, or how happy, but more than anything how much fear will come with the happiness, because the happiness is simply so acute, so strong, so luminous, a happiness that so takes over your whole life, the whole meaning of your life, that you begin to be afraid it will end. That it will stop breathing. That the happiness will forget, just once, to breathe, because at a particular moment its breathing is no longer just in a little tummy, but in a whole

94

house, a whole town. It wants to start breathing through a whole town, a whole life, and it can't be looked after anymore sitting down, in silence, at night, because it has taken wing and is now everywhere. You have to watch over it standing at the window, on the telephone, on the staircase in the house, and then on all the staircases, in all the streets. You even have to shout sometimes when you're watching over it, which makes it harder to watch over afterwards. If you get too close to it, it moves further away and you've an even bigger area to watch. If it doesn't get enough air, you're the one who begins to have difficulty breathing.

I love my son so much.

Sometimes I'm afraid he'll smash his face, or get his face smashed, or veer off the road because he's fallen asleep in his car. Sometimes I'm afraid he won't tell me everything and the idea of not knowing, of not knowing everything, cracks me up. Sometimes I'm just afraid he'll be unhappy. Because now, at his age, it would be more than a little amazing if he forgot to breathe. Normally once children get to that age, they don't forget that kind of thing anymore. They forget to ring, sometimes they forget to come home, they forget they have school, or they forget you love them, but as a rule they no longer forget to breathe. But I'm still afraid. I'm afraid he'll want to travel away to a dangerous country. I'm afraid he might hide trouble or panic from me, or some worry or other. I'm afraid some girl might break his heart, I'm afraid he won't know how to manage, I'm afraid he'll get lost, or not know anymore, I'm afraid he'll need me and won't ask for anything. I'm afraid that perhaps, for some reason I wouldn't know, he might no longer want to breathe and I'm afraid of not being there to tell him, yes, it's worth breathing, it's really worth the trouble, any trouble, any kind of trouble, it's worth the fear, worth the loss, worth all of that. That life is infinitely hard and infinitely full of light, and that the light comes from his mouth, from his mouth that keeps on breathing.

Unassumingly translated by Tom Moore

ABOUT THE TRANSLATOR
Tom Moore was born in Belfast in 1941 and educated at Royal Belfast Academical Institution and Dublin University. He pursued a career teaching languages in Coleraine, Limavady, and Antrim,

Northern Ireland. He's been married since 1969 to Ann, with four sons, the fathers of fifteen grandchildren. He is currently Chair of Examiners for A/AS French at the Council for Curriculum, Examinations, and Assessment and active in the Association of Baptist Churches in Ireland.

THE TRANSLATOR'S APPROACH
"I focussed on fidelity to the spirit and register of the original, while avoiding literalism on the one hand and personal interference on the other. I sought to provide clarity for the reader, and as much polish and elegance as possible."

16. Sunglasses

I'D LIKE TO HAVE THE TOWN all to myself.

For it to be mine every once in a while, kinda like I had booked it.

I'd like that, at times, to have the town for myself, rue Saint-Jean all to myself.

Just long enough to do my errands, say. Just long enough to live my everyday life, say, 'cause I get it that Québec City's beautiful, that it's lots of fun on the first Sundays of spring to take the minivan, leave Saint-Émile and come downtown to drive around, but it's just that me, I mean, I *live* in town and it annoys me no end to be stuck in line on rue Saint-Jean and inch forward every

98

once in a while just to go to the bank to find out I've got $23 in my account or to go to the grocery store to buy a celery stalk or to the drugstore to buy something for my pimples, just to do things everybody does every day, but that on some days I can't do like everybody else since nobody's in their own down-in-the-dumps suburb 'cause everybody's in upper town on rue Saint-Jean now.

I'd like to wear my sunglasses non-stop and I don't get why people'd judge me for that. I mean, I don't see why we get all judgmental when someone's wearing sunglasses at night, or when it's raining, or they're inside. It seems to bother lots of people, this whole sunglasses thing. I for one find this whole sunglasses thing super complicated. It seems you're hardly ever allowed to wear them in peace, it seems there are so many factors influencing whether or not you're legit with your sunglasses on, that I just feel kinda like keeping them on all the time, 'cause I feel super good with them on my face. I feel good, I feel less "there," I feel less stuck beside the people sitting at the next table at the restaurant, I feel less in the kitchen of the people I encounter at the grocery store, I feel less like I'm crying as part of a crowd watching a movie at the theater, I feel less right in the middle of the private lives of the thirty-somethings

I meet on the street as they walk their three kids in strollers and scream at each other 'cause well, christ, they made decisions that were too big too fast, too young, and now it's too bad they can't stand the sight of each other anymore and what makes 'em so upset is knowing that in theory they still have another forty years of putting up with each other ahead of them. All this to say I'd really like to wear my sunglasses non-stop. Whenever I like, you know.

I'd like that too, if we could come up with clear social codes, like "I'm available to talk with anybody and be personable" codes and "Nope, I don't think I feel like having anyone talking to me, especially if we don't know each other" codes. So that whenever I have headphones in my ears 'cause I'm listening to music, whenever I'm writing on my laptop in a public place and I'm not looking around, whenever I'm staring at my feet as I walk without ever looking up, people'd get it and avoid talking to me, I'm all for huge, planetwide mutual respect, and that mostly starts with the fact that we don't all have the same need to make friends, talk about our lives even if we don't really know each other, stay in touch with all the people we've encountered in our life. This includes the fact that I may look grumpy but it's something that happens, it's definitely nothing personal, nothing against you. It's no big deal, it's not like you need to do anything at all. Everything's gonna work out just fine for everybody anyway.

I often consider myself a social misfit. I make a special effort, I question myself. When I encounter people I know on the street and I act like I didn't see them, I feel super bad, I feel stupid and snobby, but deep down it's something I really don't get, why we put such pressure on ourselves, like we had signed contracts or, I dunno, like we had to love the whole world all the time, but to me it seems like I didn't sign the contract, I don't remember ever signing any-thing like some sociability contract, and I think to myself that no matter if we know each other or not, we sometimes talk to each other when the timing's right, and other times we don't talk 'cause we don't feel like it that particular time, and it could just not be a problem, we could stop wondering about it and feeling guilty. And it's also possible to just smile. I think we under-estimate smiling, but it's simple, it's fast, it's restrained but at the same time very warm, it means what it means. So maybe we could just smile sometimes instead of stopping and going through the same old thing every time; the same boring question that can't be answered sincerely in three seconds anyway, the same answer we don't give a shit about, not knowing what to say, awkwardness, losing two minutes of our lives, on our way again. We could just smile at each other and be ok with that. If we happen to meet and we see each other, we share a smile. If I sit next to you on the bus and we don't know each other and I look happy to be alone and it's not urgent, don't talk to me; smile at me.

Inerrantly translated by
Marie-Claude Plourde

ABOUT THE TRANSLATOR
Marie-Claude Plourde graduated from Université de Montréal in 2004 and is currently working on a Master's thesis at Université Laval on the translation of orality markers in a theatrical corpus. She particularly enjoys texts that pose challenging problems related to the translation of form. She's also fond of Peirce's semiotics.

THE TRANSLATOR'S APPROACH
"This text was translated trying to keep the same rhythm, the same breath as the original, all while staying as literally close as possible to the French version without bringing in too much strangeness."

17. Rice

EVERY NEW YEAR'S EVE, I settle accounts. I look around and give thanks—in silence, to myself—for what I have, for people, for luck, for everything surrounding me. I review the year and decide what to let go of or keep in the back of my mind. I give thanks; a wonderful expression. I remember, and I say thank you.

I take a little notebook and write down everything, a list of the wonderful things that happened in 2008. I put it all in there: my stories and those of other people. Ingrid Betancourt's release. The births of Antonin, Béatrice, Aimée, Émir, Nicolas (my friends' pregnancies); the cities I visited or revisited: Lisbon, Tavira, Faro, Lagos, Paris for not very long, Tadoussac, Wells, Christmas in New York with my family. I count my days spent near the ocean: twenty-seven. I write down the names of my new friends: Alexandrine. Estelle.

I write the name of my partner, still new, still here: Antoine. Finally, Antoine. I count all the nights I've spent with him this year: 345. 257 more than last year. I close my eyes and I think about where I was before I met him. I consider myself blessed.

I think about Barack Obama, too, and the fact that I witnessed his election on TV with my best friend, who just happened to be in Québec City for work. I think about how we said we'll be able to tell our children we were together for this historic moment; I think about the plane that landed in the Hudson River and how all the passengers survived; I think of the movies, the books, the words that came into my life and made it better, kinder, or more human; I think about Miron, whom I'd never read before and whose writing I'm now trying to memorize; I think about everyone who makes the world more bearable, and I write down their names. I think about my friends. My sister and my brothers. My parents. I also think about the recipes I learned: caramelized pineapple with honey and vanilla, cod with lemon and olives, snow crab—I had *never* eaten fresh snow crab before; I'm giving thanks for everything: recyclable paint, the color "cotton"; tofu burgers from Crac; *Communauto*; there's nothing too small. As soon as I'm done, I feel wild with gratitude.

So now I turn to my other notebook. The one I've had since I took a trip to Asia, alone for seven aimless months eight years ago. I was thirty and I didn't know anything except that I felt like rice paddies and long morning walks through the humid air with sandals on my feet, hot nights and fans, rides in mototaxis through Hanoi, plants I couldn't identify, a foreign language churning in my ears. I needed beauty and time. I needed to take the train. And I did.

I fell in love with the country first, and then with him not long after. It was a foolish and necessary love because it became the love that saved me from everything: from boredom and despair; from losing all feeling, losing myself. It was the love that couldn't be, and the love that affected me the most deeply, the most wonderful and useful love of my life—the love that taught me how to love and (because I needed to learn it) that I could be loved, loved like crazy, loved with abandon, loved more than anything else. More than seemed real. And that I could love, too, more than seemed real. Me, the person who believed I could no longer love; me, who thought I was condemned to love only crazy or unavailable men. After seven months, I came home. A few times we wrote agonizing letters to each other in English. I went back to see him twice. I cried each time I left. I felt like I was leaving the only person on earth who really cared about me. Then one day I decided not to go back. I decided, because I wasn't going to take him from his life there, and I wasn't ready to go live with him forever, that I would stay here, and I would allow myself to build a life.

Two years later I fell in love.

There is still a grain of rice in my heart. Inside the grain of rice, there's a me and a him. A parallel life in which we got married and live in Hanoi with two almond-eyed children. When I settle my accounts each New Year's, I remind myself of how old they would be. Six and three-and-a-half. One boy, one girl. With black hair and blue eyes. Each year, when I settle accounts, I give thanks for the day the grain of rice took root in my life.

Intently translated by Anna Matthews

ABOUT THE TRANSLATOR

Anna Matthews is a writer and translator based in Minneapolis. She holds an MA in Literary Translation Studies from the University of Rochester. Her creative areas of interest include translating literature from Quebec, particularly women's voices, and writing genre-free prose.

THE TRANSLATOR'S APPROACH

"When I was reading and translating 'Riz,' I was captured by the way the prose's insistent, earnest passion produced the same sort of warmth in the reader (me) that practicing gratitude does in real life. My goal was to capture the energy of the story's lists and emotion in English with careful attention to the way punctuation and voice propel the narration."

18. Knives

I AM TRYING to pretend this isn't happening to me, but it's not easy. It's like being in a fugue state, except I know that it's completely useless, like making a parachute out of bed sheets to escape a house on fire. I feel ridiculous, yet I am still doing it. I can't think of anything better.

Observing nature, a colour or a light, I try not to tell myself, "This might be the last time you see this, so save it, save it somewhere inside yourself so that you can return to it later." I am trying not to create a cemetery inside myself for everything I find beautiful, for everything I've ever found beautiful, except the closer I get to my time being up, the more I discover new things I find beautiful. I feel like I am drunk on beauty, though not happy-drunk, just sad-drunk, just really fucking sad-drunk on beauty.

I haven't told anyone.

When I think about...

Spending my summers at the lake. The water in the morning shining like a mirror and covered by a fine mist that makes you think, "My God, the birth of the universe must have looked like this." Pink and frozen in time. The gorgeous morning pink, my pink fingers at dawn, with trees that look like they're actually breathing. The sun rising. It was all so magnificent that it often made me feel like I hadn't seen nearly enough sunrises in my life. What had I been so busy doing instead of watching the sun rise every day?

When I think about that, or my garden, the heads of lettuce growing, how discreetly pretty a head of lettuce growing is, except no one notices its beautiful shades of green, the little flowers that pop up, or the raspberries, the spicy red of a raspberry sweltering in the sun, when I think about the river, in the winter, the ice, the geese on the river banks, when I think about all of Charlevoix, I just freak out. The road. L'Isle-aux-Coudres. The tip of the island. The water and the mud, the clay, its rich gray colour, and the great blue herons standing in the middle of all of this, standing in a kind of peace that you can't find anywhere else, standing in the soft atmosphere that peace creates.

I was very happy there. I was happy often in my life.

The paintings of Jean Paul Lemieux. The paintings of Riopelle.

The sea.

The fires by the shore. The sky.

My daughter's face. My God! My daughter's eyes.

I can't drive anymore. There's nowhere for me to escape. Soon, I won't be able to read anymore. I remember, when I learned how to read, I experienced a rare type of joy, one I had difficulty finding anywhere else after. I was a lonely child. I still remember telling myself, "I'll never be alone again." And here I am now, alone again.

None of this is for me anymore. I can't get it through my head, that none of this is for me anymore, not for me anymore. Museums, nature, faces, all the things that cheered me up when I felt bad about human stupidity. Forests. Books. None of this is for me anymore.

Smiles.

I am going blind.

I don't know how to do this. How to quit. This.

I've ordered two Faka throwing knives.

Instead of spending whatever time I have left being able to see and obsessing over a beauty that's driving me crazy, a beauty that's tearing me apart because I know that one day it'll end, I have decided to focus on a target. I have decided to teach myself how to throw knives so that I can offer my soul and make it stronger by sacrificing it to the cruel wolves of existence. I am going blind, which seems so unfair when you consider how much joy I get simply from looking at people, from looking at the light. I don't want to go crazy. I am going to throw knives. In the dark if I have to. That's what's going to keep me alive. Throwing knives so that the dark doesn't turn on me and swallow me whole.

I am going to throw knives and maybe once I am blind, I'll be better able to see all the secrets hidden in the beauty around me.

Nervously translated by Guillaume Morissette

ABOUT THE TRANSLATOR

Guillaume Morissette is the author of *New Tab* (Véhicule Press, 2014), which was a finalist for the 2015 Amazon.ca First Novel Award. His work has appeared in *Maisonneuve Magazine*, *Little Brother Magazine*, *Vice*, *Electric Literature*, *The Quietus*, and many other publications. He lives in Montreal.

THE TRANSLATOR'S APPROACH

"I grew up in Jonquière, Québec. French is my mother tongue, but I write and function primarily in English these days, so my life always feels to me like some sort of ongoing creative translation project like this one. My strategy to translate the piece I was assigned involved writing two drafts. My first draft was an almost word-for-word translation that felt sort of mechanical and emotionally hollow to me, like a plastic Christmas tree. I wrote the second draft a few weeks later by going over my translation and modifying the sentences simply to make them feel right to me, without allowing myself to look at the original story in French. The story I worked on features a protagonist who's going blind, and so translating in this way, without looking at the original after my first draft, felt like a kind of blindness, which seemed appropriate for this piece."

19. Trolls

I'VE BECOME scatterbrained...

It's really strange because over time I've become scatterbrained. I've become more "off-the-cuff." I've lost a lot of my attention to detail, I'm not a perfectionist anymore. I say this because before, until I was maybe... I don't know... twelve or thirteen or fourteen years old, doesn't matter, I was excessively meticulous and precise... I guess I needed that order, everywhere. Everywhere, but never as much as on top of the bookcase in my room. I had an impressive collection of trolls on display up there. They were all the rage at the time. I loved sitting on my bed staring at them, the hundred and fifteen or so of them, standing, always colourful and grinning, the bigger ones at the back, smaller at the front. There were some with diamonds in their belly buttons (that's really strange if you think about it), some with an '80s look, some from the army, nurses and doctors, sunshine trolls, married trolls. I had giant ones, I had stuffed ones, ones made out of cookies, ones that were backpacks. I had a troll bank, too. I honestly had one for every taste and I was really super proud of my collection. Of course, my whole family, every Christmas and every birthday, and sometimes also just for the hell of it, made a contribution to the ridiculously absurd accumulation of those green-haired things. I remember one afternoon I came home for lunch and my mom had left a box on the table with six little trolls in it. The ones with the '80s look... I remember the morning of my eighth birthday when I woke up with a new stuffed animal in my arms (never anything but a troll!).

And I also remember *that* afternoon.

No.

I've been talking about trolls, but I haven't mentioned the most important part; I had a grandmother who called me her best bud. She was wonderful and I loved her. She was my friend, my confidante. She made me laugh and she is still to this day the one who treated me with the gentlest and most convincing affection I've ever felt. She lived in Chicoutimi, and me in Quebec City, and for a long time we would go to the Saguenay every weekend. Friday mornings my mom would pack me a suitcase full of clothes, while I would pack my "real" suitcase, my black plastic one, the one where I would pack my favourite things, my new books, my music, things I'd made, that kind of stuff. It was so I could show it all to her, to my grandma. Today, looking back, I realize how patient she was. Because, every Friday evening, she would get stuck with a suitcase-unpacking session, commentary and feedback for every new trinket included.

There, I told you about my grandmother Nicole. *Voilà*!

Now.
That afternoon.

I was eleven years old. I was at home, in the bathroom with my mom who was cleaning the shower when, surprise, surprise, my grand-father arrived with my grandmother. What's great about being a kid is how you don't need to put all your emotions and feelings into words. It's true, and it's a shame that that's yet another thing we lose as we grow older. We're here, we're fine, we're happy, pleased, surprised and smiling. We kiss, we hug, we kiss again, we hug harder and we say nothing. Because there's no point talking, it doesn't feel as good. What a joy it is now, to stand there, in front of someone, and say, "I'm happy to see you." It's nice, it's simple, it's restrained, you can take it to the bank, but it doesn't feel as good as knocking someone over by pouncing on them. I didn't go as far as knocking my grandmother over that time, but I did hug her really, really hard just the same. Her smile was blank, her hands were less adept on my back, her eyes more resolute. She had something for me that would bring that famous troll collection to an end. It was a magnificent stuffed troll, not too big. To me it looked like a new kind of troll, its face less naïve. It was a troll that was more on edge, more bitter, more tired maybe. And there were candies inside of it. Candies that, a few minutes later in the living room, I had officially declared the best candies I'd ever eaten.

While their flavour, their colour

    while the texture of the fabric on my
hands

    while I sat on the floor facing the couch

    and the sun heated my back

    while all those sensations ran their
course through me

    while surprise and happiness and well-
being were still running their course through me

I found out that my grandmother had cancer.

I could hear my mom.

Her voice and her tears also ran through me.

That was my first contact with cancer and
also with the idea of death.

And what has left the biggest impression
on me is that things like that never leave you
afterwards.

For me, now cancer tastes like candies.

For me, tons of things are without flavour,
without sensation, without texture. Tons of
banal things, though, for me, refer to things
that are way too serious, way too dramatic. For
me, the word *blood*, for example, conjures up
war, murder. Yet there is blood everywhere in
me. The word *airplane* conjures up disappear-
ances, of that image of having to eat the flesh of a
corpse, lost in the mountains. But I love to travel.

Why am I saying this?

I'm saying this because, on the other hand, the word *cancer*, a terrible word, makes me think of something completely banal, makes me think of little pink candies, the size of a USB key, kind of shaped to look like a troll.

I'm saying this because now there's no way I can eat candies, but I'm obsessed with the flavour, with the same precision I had when I used to place my trolls on the bookcase in my room.

I think there isn't anything as precise as that left in me now.

Enthusiastically translated by Benjamin Hedley

ABOUT THE TRANSLATOR
Benjamin Hedley's childhood as a military brat exposed him to life in various places, from British Columbia to Quebec and Germany. An intense interest in literature and culture, as well as a trilingual upbringing have driven him to pursue a difficult yet gratifying career as a literary translator.

THE TRANSLATOR'S APPROACH
"To translate this short story I tried to get in the head of the narrator, to feel the loss of a loved one. I also thought back to the troll craze of the eighties and nineties, the early years of my life."

20. Dishes

IN THE MORNING, I get up, and honestly, I tell myself, this is it. I'm finally going to do it, begin, you know, get to it, I dunno. Write. At long last. I tell myself it's possible, that this might be the day, like when I turn my computer on late at night after an exultant evening, at the beginning of spring or at the first snowfall, when everything outside is like a movie, you think crazy thoughts, sublime thoughts, you tell yourself that we too could be sublime. It wouldn't be too hard, at least not so hard as we think, something extraordinary could happen to us, but in the end, nope. That's what's so awful. In the end, not only does nothing ever happen, but also, we don't make anything happen. We can't just wait, I know that, but I just don't know how to start. Where to start. It seems that at twenty I'd have known. More or less. But those days are behind me now and it's like I don't know how to do anything anymore.

In the morning, I get out of bed. I eat my breakfast, cut up some fruit, drink filtered coffee, and I like that. I listen to the radio but just sometimes. I make some toast, I do the dishes, I like doing that, I feel I'm being useful. The dishes are good because the goal is clear and easy to hit. After breakfast and the dishes, I turn my computer on and go to page 1 of the document, and that's when I think about it, though not for long, that's when I give up, because I'm struck dumb by all the emptiness I contain, because I'm as if hypnotized by defeats that haven't occurred yet. I go to my computer and instead of beginning, instead of writing a sentence, even just one, just a single line... I play a game of Solitaire. I find the name of the game hilarious, by the way. I play Freecell. I play *Questions for a Champion*. I am a champion. I read a random article on Wikipedia. I type my name into Google. I go on Facebook and invent a mysterious status for myself. I spy on people, I reply with sophistication to some of my friends' announcements.

I have the best friends in the world. Not on Facebook, in real life. They're great, and they think I'm just as great as they are. They believe me when I tell them about my day, when I tell them how my book project's coming along, when I tell them about my story. They think I'm brilliant, what with my survivors of the airplane crash, their crossed fates that never meet, the opera singer whose dad is deaf, the East German woman who makes it over the Wall with her family, the Danube, the Amerindian reserves and the string instruments, the land surveyor who writes poems, because poetry is the quest for the exact location of his own limits, where I end, where the rest of the world begins, etc. I'm unbeatable at my own game. I'm unbeatable at Solitaire, at Freecell, at *Questions for a Champion*, and at talking about things that don't exist.

I talk on the phone with Franck. I make him laugh. He's kind and nice. He is in a funk but that doesn't scare me. To the contrary. I prefer it. He never asks questions. He's in a state where people exist by virtue of what they are, not just what they do. That's rare.

I run errands, I walk in the sunlight, when the sun is out it's worse, I tell myself I've got to live and that the sun isn't always out, that I can't let myself stay holed up not doing anything important, that at least the sunlight is bright. You go out, you walk in the sunlight, it's like the dishes, the result is clear and impossible to mess up. On grey days I don't go out, I watch TV instead. I read blogs. I make roast beef and mashed potatoes. When it's nice out, I get dressed, put on some makeup, I go have a coffee at Claudette's or a glass at Bily's. I talk to people I don't know. They look at me with admiration, and it's torture.

Hell is being the only person to truly know yourself. Hell is other people's kindness, others who don't see you as you are, afraid and defeated, shaking, and imagine you a thousand times better off than you are. As a great writer, or something.

I once heard an author on the radio saying that to write is to spend much of the time not writing. I don't know about him, but I find that intolerable. Unlivable. But then I'm not a real novelist, maybe there's the difference.

Everybody thinks I'm writing the best novel in the world. Nobody knows that I don't write. Everybody believes I'm an author, but me.

Familiarly translated by Jacob Siefring

ABOUT THE TRANSLATOR

Jacob Siefring is a Canadian-American translator. His published translations include *The Major Refutation* by Pierre Senges and Stéphane Mallarmé's long typographical poem *A Roll of the Dice Will Never Abolish Chance.*

THE TRANSLATOR'S APPROACH

"In 'Dishes,' which is essentially a short monologue, I tried hard to reproduce the familiar, seemingly off-the-cuff quality of the original. The challenge was to do so while conveying its laconic, slightly ironic style."

21. Home

THE HOUSE I GREW UP in is like a tree house, only without the tree. It's as cute as can be, and whenever you look at it, you'd swear it had shot up like a mushroom, with bumps and lumps everywhere and looking a bit like a trailer, only much too big and without the wheels.

It wasn't in the best shape when we first moved in... to be honest, it was rotting on all sides. There were holes in the roof, and I'm not sure if I actually remember or if I was told about it, but the wood in the walls was so soft you could pull the nails out with your fingers.

My dad did it all up himself. Lots of times. The roof alone I think we did four or five times. The front had to be knocked down and for almost a month we lived without the front wall, like in a dollhouse, with the rooms open to the street. My dad gradually learned how to drywall and pass the wires for the electricity through the walls, and he did it. My mom breastfed my brothers on the roof, my dad balanced on the edge of the gutters, they didn't tie themselves to anything, they didn't use sunblock, they were the same age as I am now and they already had three kids, a house that was leaking every which way with hidden defects and no hope of compensation, but they seemed invincible or something, they had worked out how to live, they got stuck in, my mom was at school, my dad was juggling three jobs on top of patching all the holes, it was in shambles and it was magnificent.

I was a serious little thing, always with my nose in a book, but my brothers were natural catastrophes unto themselves, let loose on the tools and the tarp. We were forever losing one. We all regularly split open our chins, or fell, or had a brick accidentally fall on our heads, or we bled, or broke our noses, or lost a toenail in the door, especially us kids. Mom says she would be out with the twins in the stroller and other women would think she was beating them. They always had a bandage over one eye or around their heads. They were tiny and really beat up, but they climbed all over the place. What can you do? When the parents are always climbing, the kids do the same.

The whole family felt right at home there, everything was great, all was well in the world. We kept moving the rooms around. The claw-foot tub stayed in the middle of the bathroom for months and we had to walk around it to brush our teeth. I slept in the dining room for close to a year, I don't really remember why. And four rooms in the house were, at one time or other, my bedroom.

Dad also grew sunflowers, elms, and spruce trees. The backyard was like a virgin forest full of miracles and things to trip over, and there were currant bushes, tulips, lilacs, blue plums, and raspberries as far as the eye could see. I honestly believe we could have lived just off that.

We kept two turkeys, we took in an injured gull, we had a manic-depressive budgie, and later a disgusting iguana. The place was a complete and utter mess. Honestly.

There was a wonderful florist as well, near my school, who came from Lebanon and would let me buy flowers for my parents with pennies and chocolate money. Whenever Valentine's Day came round, I would buy flowers like this from the florist who lost money but would let me express my love, all my love, my boundless love for my boundless parents.

Today it's nothing at all like that. The house is always quiet, everything in its place, the twins don't climb anymore, Mom has an all-white condo, and the roof will never leak again. The Japanese say that a finished house is a dead house. I liked it better the way it used to be. When the house was alive. I'd like my parents to get back together. They were the house.

Instinctively translated by
Peter McCambridge

ABOUT THE TRANSLATOR

Originally from Ireland, Peter McCambridge holds a BA in modern languages from Cambridge University, England, and has lived in Quebec City since 2003. He runs Québec Reads and now QC Fiction, a new imprint of Quebec fiction in translation. He has translated seven novels, all from Quebec, and edited this book.

THE TRANSLATOR'S APPROACH

"Whenever I translate, whatever I want to put down in English usually comes to me pretty quickly. I either know or I don't. I like it or I'm not happy with it. Often I'll find myself translating something I suddenly realize I translated part of months earlier. I'll go back to my original translation and discover I've put exactly the same thing, word for word, the second time round too. This particular translation first appeared in Cosmonauts Avenue. I'm happy to leave the expression 'in shambles' in there. It's something their editors put in, an expression I'd never seen before and will probably never use again. But a nice reminder that any translation is a series of decisions, not all of them made by the translator. Not all of them instinctively, anyway."

22. Ice

I TAKE ADVANTAGE OF THE NIGHT TO CRY.
Night.
Blue.
And cold.
I wouldn't want to be a bat or a werewolf, but I really feel like they understand that the night is perfect for screaming.
And for biting.

I don't sleep.
At all.
I don't give a damn about sleeping.
I need to cry.

I sleep in an enormous white saucer, Corelle, strong enough to withstand my twirling.

I sleep in a saucer not of china because I toss and turn, I move around at night. In my dreams, I scream.

I dream that I'm dead and then I wake up and I cry and then I don't sleep anymore. It's always the same. I put the children down to sleep, sometimes it takes two hours, I take my time.

I have them. They are mine. So I make the most of it.

I open my bedroom window, I go to bed, I fall asleep, I dream that I have died and then that's it, I wake up and I cry.

It's my time for me.

Some people smoke cigarettes, others masturbate, I cry.

That's what relaxes me the most.

Up until the age of 16, I spent all my winter breaks with an aunt I didn't like, but who had a huge piece of land with a lake and an old house that I never had time to fully explore. We fought almost every day, but I had no choice about going, it was less complicated for my parents who worked a lot at that time. (They had a small grocery store. I don't think business was too good. I remember my dad having a lot on his mind.)

When we fought, I would go outside alone to get some air. I could spend hours on the frozen lake.

Jumping on the ice.

I was fascinated by the fact there was a ton of frozen water underneath. Within me there was an unhealthy desire, more or less conscious, of finding a body under the ice, maybe that of another little girl.

Blue.

And cold.

I never found one.

A colleague of mine (I work in the old port) goes jogging every day at noon on a cleared path along the river.

Each winter, he finds several bodies, three or four, that have resurfaced and are stuck in the ice.

I love mornings.

I never drink coffee.

But I make some every morning.

The smell.

The smell of coffee in the morning brings me great comfort.

I go and buy some every day at the café because I want it to be fresh.

I want it fresh. I want it to smell fresh.

I stop to buy croissants.

The children hate croissants.

But I need these routines.

I make sandwiches.

Three.

One for me.

I eat the same thing as the children, I always make myself the same lunch as the children.

Sandwich.

Small Oasis juice.

Fruit. Or apple sauce.

Granola bar.

In the morning, at work, I eat my granola bar standing, in front of the window that looks out onto the river, onto the pier.

And I wait to see someone jump.

I have been obsessed for years with this story of jogging and bodies in the ice.

And I'm never the one that finds them.

It pisses me off.

In the afternoon, I eat my piece of fruit. Or my apple sauce. Standing in front of the window. And I wait.

I've thought about how one day, it's me that would be pulled from the ice.

Blue. And cold.

Blue.

And cold.

Before, I took the cleared path along the river, to get home in the evening.

I took a detour.

But it was important to me.

And I would stop.

Each time.

And I was nervous.

My hands would get damp.

My breath caught in my throat.

I had my hands on the railing. Eyes closed. I bit my lip.

I bit my lip while standing on the tips of my toes.

Now, after work, I go get the children at school.

I think they're beautiful.

I never take the cleared path along the river.

But at night I cry.

Window open. Especially in winter.

Blue.

And cold.

Conscientiously translated by Michèle Thibeau

ABOUT THE TRANSLATOR

Translation, navigating words and their multiple meanings, has been part of life for Michèle Thibeau since she moved to Quebec City in the early 1990s. Michèle had an opportunity to practice French-to-English translation while at the *Quebec Chronicle-Telegraph*. She continues to dabble, in addition to writing poems and short stories.

THE TRANSLATOR'S APPROACH

"It was crucial to convey the voice of the story's main character and to capture the rhythm, emotion and stark images. I strove to remain true to the sense of poetry within this work."

23. Looks

I'VE NEVER FELT like being the non-intellectual in a family of teachers made my parents love me any less or anything. I've never felt like it mattered.

I didn't read much when I was little but my sisters did. My sisters were bright students. Just brilliant. I'd have loved to read too, but I think I was maybe a bit dyslexic or something, or maybe just not that interested. Novels, stories, literature—that's not really me. It's not what I'm looking for. I'm looking for peace. I want peace and literature is the opposite of peace. I've always been secretly jealous of people who read, because it's kind of like being a smoker: you're never alone. I don't smoke anymore so I'm alone often. But it doesn't matter.

When I was in school, I couldn't understand how anyone could listen to the teacher for such a long time. My brain looked for any possible escape. I watched the girls listening and didn't get how they did it—I didn't understand a thing. It took every ounce of energy, everything I had, just to keep still and stay in my seat. I fought this inner urge to throw myself on the ground, take off running, or head-butt the teacher in the stomach. I was going full speed on the inside with no way to let it out, so I just held it in all day to stop myself from rolling around on the ground.

I don't find girls complicated, but it was a total mystery to me how they would listen at school, so I would watch them do it, which became my way of sitting still. Their necks. Their hair. The soft skin of their wrists. Their eyelashes.

Girls are beautiful.

I learned to play football. Sure, I was too small, but it didn't matter because I was a fast runner.

I learned to fly-fish, spending hours standing silently in the water. It was like listening to the teachers, but without that urge to roll on the ground. I learned how to gut fish without a knife.

I learned to drive. I learned all the cars' names and how to repair them.

I learned birds' names. I learned how to feed them, which ones eat what and that kind of thing.

I learned to plaster and build frames. I could build a house if I wanted.

I learned butchery. A year of classes with no books. My kind of thing.

I learned to play the guitar. I learned to take photos.

I wasn't in school a long time, but I still learned a lot. After. On my own.

You can get most girls by playing the guitar and knowing all those birds' names. And you can get the rest, the really gorgeous ones, with photography. I've never been good looking, but I've always been able to get any girl I wanted.

Fly-fishing lets you go a long time by yourself without suffering.

Football, butchery, and cars let you be a part of society and find a place for yourself anywhere.

Because of everything I learned on my own, I never felt like my parents were ashamed of me, or that it mattered that I wasn't going to university or whatever. My sisters spent years at school and I didn't, but who cares? I never felt like my family of intellectuals, of teachers, was ashamed of me. And I'm the only one who knows all the rules of football and how to plaster a wall. What I'm saying is that my family accepts and respects me. And I never have any problems on the girl front either. With one exception.

But it's nothing. Really no big deal. I mean, it gets to me but it's barely worth mentioning. It's just so... I don't even know why it weighs on me so much. But when I think about it, it does.

So, yeah.

My mother has never told me that I'm handsome.

It doesn't matter, though. It doesn't really matter.

Agonizingly translated by Emily Wilson

ABOUT THE TRANSLATOR

Emily Wilson is a translator and writer mostly based in Montreal, at least when the weather's OK. When she isn't agonizing over the wording of a sentence, she's fighting Muay Thai to the death or just trying to keep her cat off the computer.

"The voice in the original story speaks in a stream-of-consciousness style with many run-on sentences and comma splices, which are much more common to French. To keep a natural-sounding voice in the translation, I had to be sure to rein in the long sentences and use a different punctuation style."

24. Notebook

I'VE ALWAYS HAD A WEAKNESS for men who write. I do a bit of writing, so I know it takes courage and a sort of self-assured humility to write, even just a little, even just for yourself. I've learned not to trust literary types, after being subjected more than once to lines like "If I weren't a novelist, I'd think I were in love with you." Lines like that really cool things down. This one guy, who kept talking non-stop, presumably to avoid kissing me, told me "In another life, this is the moment where I'd kiss you"—without the actual kiss, of course. At this point I'm over these so-called other lives and sweet lines and all that.

Still, though. Reading the writing of a man I'm in love with, will be in love with, or even just feel like I *could* fall in love with, it moves me, moves me in a way that can't be undone, takes hold of me, knocks me down. The marks on the page, the letters written so feverishly, easily, or impatiently... I'm transfixed by it. I could fall in love just like that. I'm well aware. I'm careful. I avoid book fairs, signings, and the like.

Right. That's the first thing.

The second is that I'm curious, unhealthily so, especially when I'm in love. I want to kiss everything, touch everything. I want it all, and I want it right away. I want to know the person I love. I want to love every part of them. So sometimes at the start of a relationship, I poke around. A little. Not a lot, just a little. I examine the nightstand and bottom desk drawers, the depths of the closet. The medicine cabinet. I often feel as though I'm unearthing artifacts of ancient Greece. A yearbook, a forgotten tennis racquet, travel diaries, lists of hopes and dreams, homeopathic remedies against hair loss... they tell me whole stories, everything that came before—childhood, high school, vaccinations, and crushes—everything that has inevitably led us to each other.

Antidepressants: my heart sinks. The bottle dated 1999: my heart soars.

Erotic novels. Holiday cards. Letters.

I know it's not very nice. I'm well aware that it's not okay, that I should wait until—I don't know—until I'm asked. Even though it's just so I can understand; even though it's just so I can know him more completely, the whole history of his civilization, all that has led him to me: where he came from, and what made, built, hurt, and drove him. I know that I should wait, that I'll be taken by the hand and invited into these lands when the time comes, all in due course. What can I say; I can't help myself.

Despite everything, I think it's a good thing. What I mean is that it's harmless. And it forces me to pay attention to weaknesses invisible to the naked eye. It makes me more compassion-ate—yes, that's it. It softens me.

I found a blue notebook among my ex's old things. I read it on tiptoes. I read it with my heart beating in my temples. I read the whole thing. He had written funny, loving thoughts about girls and about himself. He'd jotted down a few quotes. He wrote about his lovers. He spoke well of them, lovingly. He'd written, "When Cécile sings softly to herself as she cooks, I know I can

142

finally relax. Relax." and "M. is gone. Everything has gone dark. I'm blind again." He wrote about making love to Val, her mouth, her radiant sex. It was beautiful. He wrote about Val again, about when she went on a mission in Guatemala, her absence, and how lonely he felt. "I miss her. I miss it all," he wrote. He wrote about lovers. He wrote about girls he had wanted but never had. He wrote about a certain F. I couldn't figure out who she was, but if she had read what he really thought of her, she wouldn't have acted so superior. He wrote about all of this, his deepest feelings. I loved him for what he gave me, and I loved him for all the rest too, what was hidden in the blue journal: his past love for other girls, all his loves, those he had lived and those he dreamed of. I loved him for all of it.

We broke up, like people do when they love each other and then stop. We split up but stayed friends. One night, I went back to his place for a party. I couldn't resist: I went to see if he had written about me in the blue journal, and what he'd said.

Nothing. He'd written nothing. Nothing while we were together, or after. I hadn't left a trace.

It crushed me.

He'd written nothing. Nothing about me. As if I'd never existed. I wasn't part of his civilization.

I went back to join the others and drank rosé next to the barbeque, pretending everything was okay.

I pretended everything was okay.

Diligently translated by Aleshia Jensen

ABOUT THE TRANSLATOR
Aleshia Jensen grew up in Winnipeg, Vancouver, and a few places in between. She moved to Montreal in 2007 to study translation, and now freelances from her St. Henri apartment. Her first book-length translation is forthcoming from QC Fiction in 2018.

THE TRANSLATOR'S APPROACH
"My approach for this translation: to reproduce the style while avoiding the comma splice."

25. Brothers

CHILDHOOD IS A LOST WAR. Lost over and over again. Lost a thousand times, lost to infinity.

Most of the time, people grow up and pretend to forget that savagery. The pain is too excruciating. No one wants to relive that stage of life, with its violent battles. No one wants to remember the depth of the abyss. Or the cruelty of children.

Adulthood becomes a kind of post-war, marked by all the things we say and do to get on with life. But let's admit it: kids are mean. Not meaner than adults—equally mean. When we try to remember what it was like, we can't breathe. We break into a thousand pieces. Our legs fail. We can't stand anymore.

Children are wild, and we try to tame them. We tell them to smile. We tell them to say thank you. We say, "Don't pull that girl's hair. Put your tongue back in your mouth." We call them our little angels. "Put your tongue back in your mouth, my angel. *Smile.*"

Childhood is a lost war. Of this, more than anything, I'm certain.

I grew up with a mom and half a dad. My dad worked in James Bay, but my mom didn't want to live up there because she was always cold. So she and I lived in Limoilou, in Québec City, and froze all the same. Maybe she would have died trying to live in the tundra, I don't know.

When my dad had time off, it was a big deal. He had three weeks' vacation the entire year: two weeks in the summer and one at Christmas. The rest of the time, my mom and I got along without him. At night, I pretended not to hear her cry and she pretended not to cry. Every Friday, she used to do us both up with mascara, and I didn't really like that but I let her do it because it made her happy. She did our makeup and she bought a *millefeuille*, which we shared. Like two dolls at a tea party.

Now, remembering those nights breaks my heart. My mom, alone with her daughter every single weekend of her twenties. As pretty as a fairy with her mascara, rarer than the rarest flower, and pale like an orchid. She knitted and worked hard at her hospital job, like a good girl. She taught me to be polite and called me her angel. My mother lowered her eyes when she passed a man. As stunning as any actress, and she acted like a nun. Of course, my father was good-looking, too. Handsome like Marlon Brando. His flaw was that he wasn't around.

I'm not sure why I'm thinking about these things. Perhaps to prove to myself that I haven't forgotten. That in fact, I remember it all very well. I felt so alone, back then. I was alone. I'm still alone.

There was a time when I had friends. A lot of friends—all of the neighbourhood boys. As a kid, I was a real tomboy. Aside from my mom's Friday night mascara sessions, I didn't do girls' stuff. Girls my age annoyed me. I thought they were sissies. They were too delicate, always afraid of something. They cried too much.

I preferred to play outside with the boys. I was part of the pack, and we did everything together. We rode our bikes outside every single night from May to October. We went to the *dep* to buy chips and pop, and chilled in the schoolyard. We played hockey or swam at Alex's or Marceau's. We stole carrots from Mrs. Bélanger's vegetable garden behind my house.

I was an only child. I had a mom who cried a lot and a dad three weeks out of the year. Alex, Oli, Champoux, Marceau, Ben Sirois—those boys were my brothers. We even had our own fort on the riverbank. We shared everything. For a while, it was perfect.

Then something happened, and I lost all of that. I remember it so well. School was about to let out for the summer; in three days, I would finish Grade Five. One night, in the little forest near where we lived, my friends stopped whatever they were playing. They tied me to a tree. I was bigger and stronger, but there were five of them, and they held me still and pulled the rope tight. One after another, they came up to me, pressing their mouths against mine so hard it hurt. They forced my lips apart with their tongues. I struggled like a maniac to free myself. For nothing. It didn't make a difference.

That was childhood. They were just kids. Savages.

That night, I hated my dad for being up north. I hated my mom for showing me how to put on mascara instead of showing me how to fight. I hated being a girl. That night, I hated the people I used to love most in the world. I cried. Like a girl.

The summer that followed was the longest of my life. I felt I was all grown up and truly alone, because I couldn't ride my bike anymore. Who would I ride with? My pack had abandoned me. I had no friends.

Childhood is the war you lose the day you lose your brothers.

Elegantly translated by
Carly Rosalie Vandergriendt

ABOUT THE TRANSLATOR
Carly Rosalie Vandergriendt is a Montreal-based writer, editor, and translator. Her writing has appeared in *The Malahat Review, Room, Matrix, Plenitude, Cosmonauts Avenue, Riddle Fence,* and elsewhere. She recently completed an MFA in Creative Writing through UBC's optional-residency program. Visit her at www.carlyrosalie.com or follow her on Twitter @carlyrosalie.

THE TRANSLATOR'S APPROACH
"I aimed to convey the narrator's tangible anger at the cruelties and injustices of childhood."

26. Rabbit

EVERY FALL, I want to die.

Not so much in the "not alive" sense of the word, not to that point. It's more in my skin and breathing than deep down inside. It's more a matter of light than death.

I don't want death; I want light.

But I have the crushing feeling that it's all gone, it's not coming back.

Ever.

I'm forty-two. I have a ten-year-old boy, and even though I'm usually the one who's rational enough to reassure him, say during a storm or at night, in the fall I am incapable of being an intelligent and rational adult. I turn back into an eight-year-old, I totally lose faith in life, I become hopeless, I have sincere doubts, and I'm scared, scared that spring and summer are never coming back. I'm scared it'll rain forever, that the sun is setting for the rest of my life at three in the afternoon.

They say people in Quebec talk a lot—a lot—about the weather. They say people in Quebec have nothing to say because they're constantly talking about the weather. That's crazy. People talk about the weather because it consumes more than half their lives and their strength. Because Quebecers spend half the year struggling so they don't die of misery or exhaustion or nostalgia or boredom. Well I always listen to anyone who talks about the weather, because what they're talking about is their helplessness, and I have a permanent soft spot for that.

So when September rolls around, I come undone. And my son keeps me together. He's the one who turns on the radio in the morning, who boils the water for tea, and who runs me a bath before leaving for school. He's the one who asks me to go apple picking and the one who finds the apple crisp or apple pie recipe. He's the one who makes me laugh. He's the best medicine for my weird sickness, my fall illness that is wanting to stay in bed all day long, wanting to be there, asleep, and nothing else—wanting to become one with the bed, essentially. My doctor prescribed a weird lamp, which my son turns on at breakfast, and antidepressants, which I flushed down the toilet. The lamp makes him laugh, and that's how it makes me feel better. I sit in front of the lamp, but my body isn't fooled; neon lights don't help, but my son's laugh does.

My son's the one who keeps me together and makes me feel better. He's the one who keeps me going, largely because of that time, last October, when he brought home a rabbit, a filthy rabbit he'd found in the park by the school, a rabbit with red eyes, and my son was crying uncontrollably and was so worried because the rabbit was helpless. And he said to me that we had no choice, that we had to keep it, and that's what saved me that time, that's what made me feel a bit better, that "we have no choice." Because it's nice to think that we have no choice. It feels good sometimes to tell yourself that you have no choice. It was wonderful that, at that moment, my son looked at me and just said, with all the certainty of a child, "We have no choice, Dad. It's a matter of life and death." Because sometimes it's true that it shouldn't be a question of sunshine or rain, but of life or death, that we shouldn't smile or frown because of sunshine or rain, but because it's a matter of life and death.

Now I have a son and a rabbit. They have both saved me. They have saved me enough. I promised myself that next fall, I wouldn't curl up into a ball in bed for months, that I'd turn on the radio in the morning myself, and that we'd dance in the kitchen—me, the rabbit, and my son. That we'd bake cakes, we'd invite Jules's friends to sleep over and watch funny movies all night long with the rabbit, that we'd go swimming, walk in the park, see my parents...

Because my son and my rabbit are small and sweet and the light I was missing, that I'd given up on—I wasn't looking for that light in the right place. The light comes from my son. I don't know how I managed to stop seeing it.

Thoughtfully translated by Elizabeth West

ABOUT THE TRANSLATOR
Elizabeth West is a French-to-English translator and editor based in Quebec City. Her early love affair with words, leading to bachelor's degrees

in French and English literature and translation from the Universities of Toronto and Ottawa, has resulted in this first foray into literary translation.

THE TRANSLATOR'S APPROACH
"I strove to convey not only what the French says, but also how it says it—with the rhythm and cadence of the original prose."

27. Cinema

IN THE RICHARD DESJARDINS SONG, the girl says, "All my being wants you to be the last." It's beautiful. It's a magnificent line. I hope I'll want to say it to somebody one day. It's one of the most beautiful songs I know. When the song ends, you don't know if the guy was really the last, because it's the beginning of their life together, and she's just giving birth to their first baby when at the end she says, "Love me. Help me." You can assume that yes, the guy was the last, since this is back when you could cross the Bering Strait by foot, and relationships were maybe less complicated in those days. At the same time, maybe not. It's pretty hard to tell. But considering that life expectancy must have been around thirty-seven, you can assume that it was easier to stay with the same person your whole life.

When I was a teenager I read a lot, a lot of books that weren't meant for my young, impressionable soul at all. I read everything I came across. At twelve or thirteen, I was reading the Countess of Ségur and Stephen King, but also things like *The Unbearable Lightness of Being* and *Anna Karenina*. I read a lot of books that weren't meant for my age, sometimes only half understanding them, but still. That's how, in my little head, I quietly created an image of love that, when it was true love, couldn't be, that had to be fought for, that wasn't quiet, calm or happy, that was full of inner upheavals and premonitions of revolution, full of scrapes, melancholy, tears, train stations, torn skies, storms, ultimatums, long sad letters—full of everything that seems like real life when you're a teenager and you read late into the night, under the covers with a flashlight, all alone in your childhood bed in the big family home.

You're so bored at thirteen. The boredom is almost metaphysical. You swear to yourself that you won't always be bored like this.

I was also obsessed with a French film that I watched every Tuesday the summer I was thirteen or fourteen. It was the summer it cost just sixty-seven cents at Blockbuster to rent an art film (the movie was French, so it was an art film, even if it was a stupid romantic comedy), and so I got to watch my movie every Tuesday of the summer. That's about thirteen Tuesdays.

I'm embarrassed to say what the movie was. My only excuse is that I was fourteen years old.

Okay.

I watched *Fanfan*, a film based on a novel by Alexandre Jardin, some twenty times that year. It had Sophie Marceau and... shit I forget his name. Alexandre. Antoine. Crap. A French actor, anyway. This is so annoying. Vitez. This sucks. Perez! Vincent Perez.

In the movie, as in the book, the guy is engaged to a girl, and he falls in love with another woman, but he decides to stay with the one he doesn't love anymore in order to preserve his new love from the everyday, so that the passion between him and Fanfan, Sophie Marceau, will last forever. He gives her lots of wonderful moments. He puts sleeping pills in her drink the evening he tells her that he really sees her as a younger sister (which is false), and he takes her to the sea while she sleeps, and she wakes up in front of the ocean. He takes her dancing on a set of Vienna, in an empty film studio at night. He takes her into attics. He breaks into luxurious apartments with her. In short, he makes her fall madly in love and he refuses to consummate and he stays with the other woman. Until Sophie Marceau flips out. And I don't remember how things work out, but they break a mirror at the end and they're finally reunited and when you're fourteen, you cry. You go to sleep in your childhood bed and you dream of a great, complicated, romantic love. You don't know yet that you have to be careful what you wish for, because usually you end up getting it.

I got my great complicated love. I was twenty years old and I got my beautiful love, my great love, my beautiful novel, my cinema story. I got the ultimatums and the long sad letters, but also the summer nights sleeping outdoors or making love on the roof. I got the fireworks, the first snows, the sunrises. I got all that, you know. Then it ended, because it couldn't really be, because it was complicated for real.

He was so perfect and he hurt me so much.

I haven't been in love in years. I'm scared it'll never happen to me again.

I can't believe, I can't believe it will never happen to me again, but suddenly, I'm scared of never falling in love again.

I'm scared that he was, in spite of it all, the last.

Competently translated by Riteba McCallum

ABOUT THE TRANSLATOR
Riteba McCallum lives in Montreal and works as a freelance translator.

THE TRANSLATOR'S APPROACH
"I stuck closely to the literal text while trying to preserve the narrator's conversational tone."

28. Constellation

WHAT REALLY FREAKS ME OUT is the thought that things will stay the way they are forever.

Back then, I didn't want to own anything, I refused to buy a single piece of furniture. I wanted to be able to go away at the drop of a hat, without having to justify or find a home for or organize anything. I didn't want to be tied down in any way. It was a bit extreme. Now I do have some furniture. Not that much, but still. Finally, I didn't even go away that often. I wanted to be able to go away, which is a different thing. I realize now that the ability to leave is in your head. Furniture is hardly ever the issue.

I did travel some. The way people do, the way lots of people my age do, anyway. I like travelling. Being pulled out of my life. Uprooted. I like travelling alone and ending up somewhere where nobody knows a thing about me and I could be anybody, be everything I can't be here. It's mind-blowing to arrive somewhere and say to myself: "This could be the place." I could slip away, leave everything behind, leave Quebec City, what's keeping me there finally... People? People. O.K. But what if I got really tired, one day? What if I felt exhausted, if I felt I had been going around in circles for too long, if I felt stuck here, what if in the end there was nobody here for me? I could go away. To a little town in the south of Portugal. I'd arrive like a witch and move into a place on the second floor where the windows would always stand wide open. With a white, white bed in the middle of the room, with linen sheets, a wooden table, two chairs and the rest completely bare. A few dresses, books, pretty curtains. I could get up early and go down to the port to buy fish. Strike up an acquaintance with the fishermen. Ask them how their wives were doing. I could work in the mornings in a café run by my new friends from France, do my grammar exercises in my little Portuguese notebook, serve up glasses of cold watermelon juice mixed with ginja. Wash the dishes outside, cook shellfish. I could write in the afternoon, or give massages to tourists. It would all be so easy. I could have a blue-eyed child who would speak two or three languages and know how to swim. I could learn the names of the local birds and plants. And celebrate Christmas.

Nobody would ever know.

I have nothing to hide. It's just that at some point, people know you, or they think they do: they've got their image of you, their neat little summary of you, they tell themselves that you're complicated or naïve, that you read a lot, you're not funny or you're short on patience, you're so nice that you're a pushover, you have sex with too many guys, you don't know what you want, you want too much or not enough, you're an opportunist or you lack ambition, you're moody or absent-minded or a control freak, you're a hypochondriac, you're a feminist, you're motherly, you're envious, you're poetic, and it's true, or it isn't, and it doesn't really matter: the fact is that you become what other people think you are, and that, way more and way more effectively than owning furniture, is what ties you down.

That's why I like to travel alone. Why it makes my head spin to think I could start over again somewhere else, and live a totally different life.

That's another wonderful thing: all those other lives, those dream lives shining there in the darkness like a multitude of tiny beacons, like a constellation made of everything we could be. If things are not going your way where you're living, if that life has lost its appeal for you, you can always come here, there are always lights shining, always. When I close my eyes, I see the light from those small bright windows flickering everywhere on the planet.

Tavira. That's the name of that little Portuguese town. Tavira.

As a child, I dreamed of moving, changing schools and being the new girl in class. Sometimes, these days, I still dream of that, I still dream of a place where nobody knows me and I could be new again.

But.

Finally, my biggest dream now is that one day, I'll feel the desire to take root somewhere.

Sensitively translated by Lori Saint-Martin

ABOUT THE TRANSLATOR

Lori Saint-Martin is a professor in the Département d'études littéraires, Université du Québec
à Montréal. With Paul Gagné, she has translated
over 90 books from English to French, winning 3 Governor General's Awards and 4 QWF
Translation Prizes. She also translates from
Spanish to French and self-translates from French
to English. She enjoys moving between two native
languages, one of which she learned in her late
teens. She is the author of four works of fiction,
including a novel, *Les portes closes,* incomparably
translated by the one and only Peter McCambridge.

THE TRANSLATOR'S APPROACH

"I read the piece about 786 times, a couple of times
out loud, mentally thinking of avenues without
writing anything down; then I did a really fast,
intuitive draft as if writing it creatively myself (it
helps that I have written stories that cover basically the same terrain), put it aside, and rewrote
it three more times, pulling it back closer to the
original sometimes, sometimes a bit further away
to boomerang it back closer. About 20% of what
is in my final version was there in my first draft."

29. Flood

SKIN. It's hard to explain.

I have soft skin, I've been told that a lot, people have said as they've touched it that my skin is like honey, and I believe it, I can believe it, anyway how would I know whether or not it's true—skin is soft to others, not to yourself. But I still think that skin is not soft on its own, there's nothing objective or verifiable about its softness because in order to be soft it's got to rub against some other skin and it's there, it's in that friction of those two skins that softness is created, softness exists between them. Skin is soft for two. Or softness itself is imagined.

I think our skin lives a life that doesn't belong to us. I think we submit ourselves to its humours, to its goodness, to its clemency, to its patience, or its impatience. To its fixed ideas. To its obsessions.

I'm not my skin. But I inhabit it. I live with it.

When I started going out with Phil, I was completely submersed in my skin, in my skin that wanted his skin. We worked together at an agency and one night, after months of brushing against one another, during a heat wave, we threw ourselves at each other. We were doing overtime so we could be together at the office because we were so very productive during the time when we circled one another and we weren't at all afterwards. But we couldn't have cared less. Starting from the moment when we finally kissed, from the night that followed, we didn't stop making love for weeks. It was all we did. We would get together in the evenings and make love before supper and start up again afterwards, we would wake up at night and our bodies had almost begun to make love of their own accord, we made love while we slept, we made love in the morning when we woke up, even if we didn't want to. We were overtaken by our desire, our eyes were shadowed, we were besieged by the violent and constant, constant wanting of our skins. We made love at work, we made love at the movies, we made love in the car, in restaurant bathrooms. Once we even got a ticket because we'd started to make love in a park, we were right behind a police station, we knew it was stupid of us but we laughed, we laughed and we went home to make love again, our desire for one another knew no end. I asked myself if you could make love too much. If what we were doing was even physically possible. I've never experienced anything like it with anyone else, such a thirst for someone, neither before nor afterwards. Like a forest fire. Like great tides, or spring floods. Nothing could stop it, it was impossible to act against it, it was what it was, and we had no say in it, we could only follow the current and the current pushed us against each other several times a day, every day. We couldn't believe it. I was afraid it would exhaust itself but no, it continued, and I loved all of it, his arms around me, his hand between my legs at night, his back, his hands, his hands, his hands, his hair, his skin. My skin loved his skin. His smell calmed me and inflamed me at once. He washed with white soap, I now use the same one, when I'm falling asleep I put my nose to my elbow and I have the feeling that he's still here. I felt like he was made of gold, of liquid gold. I felt like I was rich.

When it was over I didn't understand. He was vague and categorical, and I don't think you can hold people back so I let him go.

We still work together. We see each other every day. He's nice to me. I was really sad; I still am, honestly. He has a new lover now whom I've refused to meet and he lives with her. When he kissed me at Christmas my heart leapt and I thought he wanted to get back together but no, after all, no. It was just his skin. His skin still loves my skin. Nothing disgusts me more than a guy who cheats on his girlfriend while serving up some kind of bullshit soup about the present moment and all that shit. But he didn't say anything, he didn't bullshit me, he just didn't say anything. He kissed me, he put his arms around me again, and I, again, I didn't have the strength to say no, to go against our skins. I stayed and I responded to his kisses. So we started to make love again in secret, less often but just as intensely. Except now it's tearing me apart. And we never sleep together.

I often wonder why my ex lives with his new lover and why we are still lovers and I ask myself what to do and I don't know anymore. I don't know what to do.

I ask myself every day if her skin is as soft as mine. Probably. It must be. I wonder what it's like when they make love. What she did to win him. I look for a kind of answer that would take me out of here, get me out of this. Out of this defeat. Out of this flood. And I tell myself that when it comes down to it, when it really comes down to it, we've all lost.

Empathetically translated by Melissa Bull

ABOUT THE TRANSLATOR
Melissa Bull, a writer and translator from Montreal, has published fiction, non-fiction, poetry, and translations in a variety of publications. She is the editor of *Maisonneuve* magazine's "Writing from Quebec" column and the author of a book of poetry titled *Rue*. Her translation of Nelly Arcan's *Burqa of Skin* was published in 2014. Melissa currently lives in England.

THE TRANSLATOR'S APPROACH
"I just wanted to follow the author's flow of words, the speaker's trickle-to-torrent of feelings as closely as possible."

30. Pandas

I GET INCREDIBLY DEPRESSED every time I go to a suburban shopping centre. Depressed to the point of panic. They're horrible. All the stores are always on the verge of closing down, plenty of them have closed already, vacant spaces, the stores that are open are stores for old people... point is, I hate it.

I hate the Beauport mall, the Lebourgneuf mall, the Les Saules mall, the Neufchâtel mall, the Charlesbourg mall.

I detest Rossy.

Dollarama.

Buck or Two.

Giant Tiger.

They depress me.

On the other hand, I love grocery stores.

I love grocery shopping.

Except at the Super C in Neufchâtel. That place depresses me even more.

Until I was twelve or thirteen, my mom and I went grocery shopping every Thursday.

It was one of the most important things in my life. It was our date night.

A lot of things had changed in our life.

My dad left. My grandparents who lived next door to us died. So we stopped going to their place for brunch on weekends. We sold the house. I changed schools. Changed friends.

But we still kept going grocery shopping together. On Thursday.

We would eat at Super Frite. My mom would order me two *steamés* and a "hair" juice (which was more logically a peach juice, I imagine), we'd do a bit of shopping in the small shopping centre, then, finally, we'd go grocery shopping.

I was always mature. Or anxious. But in any case, I was quiet. That's why my mom brought me with her. Because I didn't say a word. She always liked that I didn't say a word.

A lot of things changed. But not that trad-ition. Not our Thursday outings.

But a lot of other things changed.

My mom changed.

But never our wonderful Thursday evenings.

I had the entire collection of *Hibou* maga-zines, which we would buy at Dollarama. My favourite was the one about pandas, I loved pandas. Now I despise them. But at the time, I went crazy whenever I saw a panda anywhere. I never saw one in real life. I probably would have had a heart attack.

Then one day, a Thursday, I saw some on a pair of pyjamas.

I saw, on those particular blue pyjamas, black and white pandas by the dozen.

We were at Rossy, we had just walked into Rossy, my mom was holding my hand, and the first thing I saw was my beautiful pyjamas. I acted like I hadn't seen anything, we went down a few aisles, I walked away from my pyjamas, then I went back to them.

When I went back to my mom, a little nerv-ous because she absolutely had to buy them for me, she was sitting in a patio chair, in a sum-mer patio display, a cheap patio set, smoking a cigarette.

My mom was committed that night.

It was my uncle who, three days later, agreed to take me to buy my pyjamas.

I wore them for three weeks without ever taking them off.

I didn't see my mom again during that time.

Then it hit me one night. I woke up in a panic. Terrified I would never see her again.

I got out of bed, left my room, then the house.

I walked. For a long time. A car stopped. I said: "I'm going to the hospital to see my mom." I got in. I was holding my pyjama top in my hands. It was damp. Sweat, probably.

I don't remember their faces anymore. But they drove me to the hospital, they went inside with me. The guard told us that visiting hours were over, so they took me back to my uncle's. I got out of the car, I don't think I said anything, I don't think I said thank you, I was... I was ripped open, a gaping wound, exposed to the black night sky. I was broken forever. I became a little different, sadder, a little more all alone forever.

My uncle woke up not long after. He came outside, then started shouting and running towards me.

I'd put my panda pyjamas on the ground and set them on fire.

I was naked, outside, in the middle of the night,
my uncle beside me, while my pyjamas burned.

One day, I'll do a documentary on pandas.
It'll talk about being bipolar,
    abandonment,
    lost traditions,
    how nothing is ever the same as it was
before,
    infinite sorrow.

Effectively translated by Cassidy Hildebrand

ABOUT THE TRANSLATOR
Cassidy Hildebrand is a freelance translator who studied translation at the University of Ottawa. She loves, in no particular order, music, movies, food, fashion, sports, travelling, reading, writing and translating. She mostly translates jargony, technical stuff, but every now and then, she's lucky enough to translate short stories.

THE TRANSLATOR'S APPROACH
"I wanted to stay true to the rhythm of the text, to the contrast between the fragments and the lingering sentences; between the blunt, pointed statements and the stream-of-consciousness-like sentences that are more wistful and poetic in nature."

31. Puberty

I ONCE BROKE A LAPTOP by throwing up on it.

I was fourteen, it was my father's first laptop, I think they cost a lot more then than they do now—actually, they were ridiculously expensive back then.

I was chatting on ICQ (MSN's predecessor) and at one point it went "uh-oh," that noise it made when you got a message. So far nothing particularly bizarre. It was my girlfriend. Still nothing too bizarre. The part I'm pretty comfortable with labelling *bizarre* starts right when she wrote to me, just like that, that it was over, I mean that she was leaving me, just like that, just fucking like that. I started to really panic, I got stressed, it all came bubbling up and then I chucked up over the screen and the keyboard of my father's computer. I shouted for him to come, he came, he shouted too, he looked at the screen, he read what was on the screen, he stopped, he said nothing, he took a moment, then he closed the computer up, he folded the screen down over the keyboard and put it in the garbage. He touched my shoulder and went out.

I was fourteen, I was in love like a dog, I was in love like a child, I would have done anything for that bitch who dumped me via ICQ, she made me humiliate myself by throwing up on my father's laptop, which must have cost him three thousand dollars, I hate her and if I ever see her again I think... Worst of all, actually, the most humiliating thing in all this, is that if I saw her again, ten years later, I think I'd want to make out, I think I would make out with her, even if she didn't want to, she would really owe me that, I reckon, because I loved her like a fool, that fucking jerk WHO DUMPED ME ON THE INTERNET, I repeat, I loved her and that time, that time when I threw up on my father's laptop, I thought I was going to die. I was sitting on the office chair, me, my twenty-seven zits and all my innocence, we were sitting nicely on the office chair, a big black chair with wheels, we were sitting on it, not hurting anyone, full of hope, me, my zits and my innocence we were doing just fine, it was really great that innocence and then all of a sudden ICQ blew up in my face, ICQ tore into me like a bull and I thought I was going to die.

I stopped getting zits, I changed, I got hairy, I became a bit nastier, more suspicious, less trusting. I started being afraid of other people, being suspicious of other people, laughing at other people. Nothing too extreme, but it wasn't there before that. All of that just wasn't there before.

Actually, that time—here I'm still talking about that fucking time I threw my puberty up on my father's laptop, I could talk about it endlessly—that time, I felt so shit, everything inside me was collapsing, I had a new opinion of myself, I realised things I'd never realised before, all my faults were displayed to me at full zoom, I felt like shit when my father came into the office, I felt like shit when my father saw that my girlfriend had just dumped me on ICQ, I felt like shit when my father put his hand on my shoulder and my instinct, the instinct I still have, is to stop taking things so seriously, to start taking things lightly, not in the zen meaning of the word, not in the "disappointed and disillusioned" sense of the word, I think I'm someone who's only a little disillusioned or not at all disillusioned, but more nonchalant, less in a rush; you might say I think it's a shame. Frankly, I have become a lighter, funnier, less sensible, more detached person, I'm the cute boy who's still a bit of a teenager, I make everyone laugh, I'm really nice, I've got loads of friends, everyone talks to me, but I think that at fourteen I was all set to become a person who was gloomier, more intense, more mysterious, a bit more complicated. Someone really happy, but more serious, more mature.

ICQ: I seek you. Wish they wouldn't seek me anymore. I'm no longer someone people need to seek, nobody needs to make me throw my guts up to get to know me anymore, there's no longer any mystery about me, I am transparent. That works really well in public, I'm totally straightforward. That's it, I'm totally straightforward. I'm totally straightforward and I'm wondering, if my girlfriend dumped me tonight on Facebook, would I even have anything left to throw up? I guess the answer is, not much.

Erratically translated by J.C. Sutcliffe

ABOUT THE TRANSLATOR
J.C. Sutcliffe is a writer and translator. She has lived in England, France, and Germany, and currently lives in Canada. Her translation of *Document 1* by François Blais will be published by BookThug in 2018.

THE TRANSLATOR'S APPROACH
"So many of the decisions about voice, style and register are based on a book as a whole, so translating this short extract without the context of the whole felt a bit like trying to slot a key into a lock while blindfolded."

32. Missiles

THE SHOWER AT OUR PLACE is barely more than a trickle. It's really unpleasant and I can't quite fathom how it's possible—in Quebec, in 2012—for there to be so little water pressure. It *is* very eco-friendly, though. Nevertheless, the trickle this morning was even more pitiful than usual. I stepped into the shower, turned on the water, and said to myself, "Christ on a bike, you'd think we were in a refugee camp or something."

That was a bit strong, I suppose. But I do tend to lay it on thick and say things that have nothing much to do with anything. This morning, I realized I don't know anything. Well, not much,

I mean. Not much at all, if you really get down to it. What I do know about stuff, about what's happening elsewhere in the world, is always what we hear about it here, twenty thousand kilometres away. Or what people say about it sixty years after the fact.

And it's rarely the truth. Or in any case, it's just a tiny fragment of the truth.

I've never known any of the "during." I've seen Berlin, I've seen Beirut, I've seen Cambodia, and I've seen Vietnam. I've seen the Huron village, and I see Quebec every day. But I saw Berlin fifteen years after 1989, I saw Beirut nearly twenty years after the civil war, and I saw Cambodia and Vietnam from a tour bus. We stuck to the safe touristy areas. I go to the Huron village for brunch more or less every Sunday morning, but I'm completely in the dark when it comes to their heritage—and yes, I do think they have a heritage. I'm a Quebecer. I love my culture and my country, and I bear within me the marks of many failures. The kind of marks you get when they've walked all over you. I bear the marks of a culture that has been downtrodden, humiliated, ridiculed. These marks are pretty much invisible, though, like they don't have any roots. I don't really know where it all comes from. We walk on autopilot, heads down, hands in our pockets, and we don't really care that much how we all came to be walking around like losers.

When I went to Berlin, the very first day, I met some people over there I really clicked with. We spent three weeks together, we went out to bars, and I came home at three in the morning completely off my face three nights a week. We picnicked in parks, we went out for coffee. It was great.

When I went to Cambodia, I did the rounds at the markets, I spent days on end visiting the floating ones, I hiked a bit in the mountains, I bought stuff for my friends, I did the beach thing, I drank tea. The language really freaked me out, so I didn't talk to anyone.

When I went to Beirut, I thought it was amazing. I thought it was an amazing city. Now, whenever I get a good whiff of garbage, it reminds me of my trip to Beirut. In a good way. And I like to breathe that smell in because it reminds me of my nice trip to Beirut.

Wherever I go, I feel like I'm at an all-in-clusive—but an all-inclusive for snobs. I think I'm being cool when I trash-talk those package trips to Cuba or the Dominican Republic, but I travel the exact same way when I go to Germany, Lebanon, and Asia. Looking for something fun, something pretty, something to take a photo of. I befriend English people in Berlin, French people in Lebanon, Americans in Asia. And I make a point of keeping in touch with them. I do talk to the locals over there. I talk to the Cambodians, the Berliners, the Lebanese—pretty much just to ask them for a coffee or whether I can use their toilet, though. It's not that I don't care. Often I'm just lazy.

I never put myself in danger.

I've never been to India, because they're still too far up shit creek. They're still too stuck in the "during" and aren't far enough into the "after"—that time when everything's back to normal.

I'd never go to Israel now because they're up to their necks in the "during."

I'd really raise my eyebrows at someone who was heading off to Afghanistan or Syria right now.

I do see tons of photos of the "during," though. I see photos of children lying on their bellies in the gutter. I see photos of boys who've lost limbs and girls who've been burned. I see photos of ruins and explosions. I see tons of photos of cities red with blood. I see tons of photos of disgusting rivers and people who are sick because they bathe in them.

But you won't see me in any of those photos. There are no photos of me bathing with them in their shitty river, no photos of me washing my laundry in there, no photos of me screaming and shouting and digging through debris to help someone find their son or their husband or their twenty-year-old girlfriend. No photos of me a whisker away from stepping on a landmine. No photos of me helping people risk their lives to sneak across to West Berlin. No photos of me amidst a crowd of protesting Tibetans. No photos of me with a Lebanese guy showing me the ruins of his decimated city, no photos of me taking him in my arms when he breaks down in tears, no photos of me crumpling to the ground with him.

No photos of me sitting in a coffee shop with a Serb telling me how he lost his mother, his wife, and two of his three daughters.

I know it's okay not to be in those photos, that I don't necessarily have to be in those photos to be a good person. But sometimes there's a little part of me that wants to open a travel agency someday.

And those who are up for it, who are ready
who are fed up of reading in the newspapers,
watching on TV
who are fed up of travelling in the "after"
who are fed up of looking at photos and figur-
ing it must be really rough for the photographer
will come.

And they'll go risk their lives to visit countries filled with tears
blood
screaming mouths
screams you can feel in your bones
deathly fear
fear of dying
violence
fleeing
nighttime
rain
wind right in your face
that smothers you
suffocates you
noise
fire
gunshots
gardens of ash
brothers who explode while holding their
hands up

row upon row of limp corpses

busloads of corpses piled on top of one another

busloads of zombies.

They will take photos

and I will have given them

tons of little flares to hand out—missiles—to launch in distress all the way over here, so we'll see them burning red in the sky and go outside and scream along with them once in a while, that's all, so it resounds far and wide and isn't all so one-sided.

So we can tear each others' throats out as well.

Curiously translated by David Warriner

ABOUT THE TRANSLATOR

David Warriner emerged largely unscathed from an Oxford education and narrowly escaped the graduate rat race by hopping on a plane to Quebec. Fifteen years into a premium commercial translation career, he listened to his heart and decided to turn his hand again to the delicate art of literary translation.

THE TRANSLATOR'S APPROACH

"This was a curious text to translate, and my challenge as translator was to convey that curiosity to the English-speaking reader. The narrator is curious to travel outside his native Quebec, but never outside his comfort zone; he senses certain things about his own identity, yet he shows no curiosity to dig beneath the surface. The choice of punctuation can be somewhat curious too, and there was a limit to just how much of that curiosity I could reflect in the English without rendering the text unreadable."

33. Tsunami

WHEN I SAW HIM THE FIRST TIME, there was no way I could've known what was going to happen to me. He was a friend of friends and he was cute, for sure, kinda. I mean like a lot of guys, like a guy you're still not sure if he's cute, y'know? He'd dressed all offbeat in repurposed clothes or something, the kind of guy that knows something about life and style, not like you, right, he looks like he's from Berlin or something. You're dressed in stuff from Simons and just don't have the time to be on-trend. You'd like to, you really would, but that style's just not made for average girls, you'd have to be gorgeous just to pull it off, know what I mean? K-Ways like when we were little, like nylon, I dunno, emerald-green, stripes, vintage Adidas, all that stuff, right, beanies, the "I come from the suburbs and I've gone back to my roots but with a slight delay so that makes me so unique and, also, socially responsible, because I don't buy anything new" type. Y'know? Those oversized glasses. Synthetic cross-body bags. Played-out. Cute, but played-out.

He was always there. He started to be there all the time. You don't know someone, you never see him, wait, no, that's not true, you've seen him but you just don't remember, because you don't know him, and now, all of a sudden, he's every-where. You run into him all the time and when you do, you realize you're really happy, I mean really a lot, and one day, this is pretty good, you talk to each other for twenty-five minutes at the corner of Saint-Jean and Salaberry, and because it's late in the day, the sun hits him right in the eyes and you think, you think, actually you don't think anything, because you're noticing the col-our of his eyes and it's like water, like something that calms you, just so amazing and you fall in, and he's talking and you are too apparently because he's responding, he's laughing, he's smiling and you also notice his smile and you think no way, listen, listen to what he's saying, one day he'll ask you about this conversation and you won't be able to answer. You won't know anything, only the colour of his eyes, only that you were immersed, that you drank, that you were thirsty for the colour of his eyes and from now on they're the only thing you know.

People think falling in love is complicated. That's not true. It's the biggest lie in the world. It's so not true and I don't know who benefits from going around saying things like that. Sure, it's rare. But it's so not complicated. There you are, at the corner of Saint-Jean and Salaberry, you're there at the corner, and the sun is setting in the eyes of this guy in front of you, and you think, this is it. This is where I want to be. It's everything.

It took going to a party with other friends for us to kiss finally, because we live in a world where kissing is apparently just as complicated as falling in love. Besides, you don't really do it on a street corner for no good reason. By the way, we're wrong about that too. We should kiss a lot more and not have to explain it all the time. Anyhow, a week later we played 'Never Have I Ever' at our friends' and we finally kissed. I thought he didn't like what I was wearing,

I thought he thought I was stuck-up, maybe he thought that and maybe he still does, it doesn't change anything and that's not the point: the point is that me and Simon Lepage made out and it was the beginning of time. Everything exploded, the water in his eyes, the room, the apartment, the city, all of Quebec exploded when we finally kissed. Everything jumped, everything blew apart, the neighbourhood, the sun, the seasons. My legs were shaking and I almost fell down. The ground began to shake and a huge wave burst out from inside our bodies and rushed out into the world and washed away everything, every single thing, and I can tell you now there's nothing that can take me back there, and what I'm saying here is important. It's that, for the second time in my life, I'm in love. I love Simon Lepage and that's an understatement. It's a miracle. And I didn't do anything to make it happen. It just happened. Like the opposite of a disaster.

Affectionately translated by Anissa Bachan

ABOUT THE TRANSLATOR

Anissa Bachan specializes in French-to-English translation. In 2014 she was hosted by the Banff International Literary Translation Centre. She is also the recipient of a Joseph Armand Bombardier Canada Graduate Scholarship (SSHRC) for her graduate research on the ideological dimensions of political translation in contemporary Quebec.

THE TRANSLATOR'S APPROACH

"I aimed to adopt the voice of a twenty-something English-speaker, while remaining faithful to her tone and the story's setting."

34. Churches

THE WHOLE WORLD tries to convince you that nothing is worthwhile and everything is pointless. Especially things like waiting, believing, and hoping. Only fools and weaklings wait, believe, and hope. And little girls. And old ladies.

I don't believe in God, as in *capital gee-oh-dee God*, but I do believe in something. I've never told anyone what that something is because that's the only way to truly keep something secret. I don't think waiting makes you a fool. I think sometimes waiting is the smartest thing to do, if you do it patiently. Don't cross off the days with bitter curses. Stay calm and peaceful and use your time in a meaningful way. Build a garden, try a soup recipe, knit a scarf, write a novel, sew a skirt, memorize some poems. Do anything, as long as you can put love into it.

You can put love into making tea every morning, having people over for dinner, reading plays, doing chores, or repainting every room in the house. The great thing is, the more love you put into things, the more you have inside you, just glowing and waiting. If God watched me sleep at night, he'd see me glowing in the dark from all the waiting. I've been so devoted, so serenely patient, and my whole body is so full of patience, it'll start pouring out soon for everyone to see.

I wait because I think waiting is beautiful. Because it's beautiful, and I like getting up every morning knowing I'm ready if he comes to me, finally. I'm totally, completely, one-hundred-percent present and absolutely ready. And I'm not disappointed when it doesn't happen. Instead, I tell myself tomorrow might be the day and I go to bed even more available, even happier and more excited about tomorrow. My hands are small and delicate and tend to fidget, but they can wait. They rest on my stomach or stay warm between my thighs, waiting for him.

Sometimes, I'll be in the middle of something, like cooking or something, cleaning or reading or looking at photos, and I feel him so strong all of a sudden, it's like it's happening now, like I just know, and I get up and wipe my hands on my apron or put the photo album down on the coffee table and I go to the door. I stand there in front of the door waiting quietly and smiling because it's finally happening. He's finally going to open the door and see me standing there, smiling and ready this time to love him and keep him with me. I know I'll be able to hold on to this one.

I'm waiting for Marc to give me a sign, and that doesn't make me a stupid, desperate little girl. It means I'm filled with hope and with faith, like a church back when churches were still full of people, and if Marc never knocks on my door or holds me in his arms, if he never gives me the sign I'm waiting for, then one day I'll put on a dress and perfume my hair the way I know he likes and I'll walk right up to his house. I won't say a word. I'll just stand there in my dress, at the bottom of the stairs, with perfume in my hair, and Marc will be inside and he'll sense that I've been waiting for him all this time. He'll come outside and when he sees my dress and smells my hair, he'll understand whatever he didn't understand before and stop being afraid of whatever he was afraid of before and he'll walk down the stairs and take me in his arms forever. And if he doesn't sense anything when I'm at the bottom of the stairs, I'll walk right in. It'll be night, and I'll see that he glows in the dark when he sleeps, and I'll just lie down beside him, quietly, and I'll let him sleep.

You can sleep all you want, Marc, but I'll be there beside you. I'll lay on top of you and touch you and watch you sleep. You can sleep all you want. You don't have to come down the stairs if you're afraid. Just let me come to you. I'll climb up to you like a Pope giving an address to say that love is real, and I can prove it. I'm a Pope, and the thing I believe in more than anything in the world is real. The fact that I have stood there, in front of my door, waiting for you, proves it's real. It is absolute proof that I'm filled with the greatest love for you. And I have been so devoted in my waiting that it calls to you. It's been calling to you a long time, and you're coming. You'll open the door and see me there, smiling, and you'll want to put your arms around me and hold me close to you forever, and we'll stay there at the door for all time, like a religion that never lost its followers.

Eventually translated by G. Lefebvre

ABOUT THE TRANSLATOR
G. Lefebvre is from Shania Twain country. He
writes and translates in Quebec City.

35. Collection

I'M A HANDSOME LAD.

An' know I'm somebody really intelligent.

Plus I'm really funny.

The people I hang out with would die for me, and believe my every word.

But I'm a complete mental defective.

I've got the direst hang-ups—the most compulsive obsessions on the planet. I could give a lecture about them. I'm a world expert on the subject. You know, I'm a dab hand at managing my compulsive-obsessive hang-ups—and a past master at the art of camouflage. Nobody has a clue my brain is completely fucked up.

I've been blessed with the biggest pack of obsessions that exist, I landed the jackpot. I've got all the blatant ones: don't walk on cracks in the pavement, don't walk under a ladder, check the burners are switched off, I always put items back in the exact same place on my bedside table, walk up and down the passage four times before going to bed, run my fingers round my eyes before going to sleep, count to six before answering the phone, squeeze my nose for four seconds when walking past a cemetery. I've got the lot. Plus I do the business like a real virtuoso. And am incredibly subtle. Not much choice about that.

An' my range also covers optional obsessions, though I never chose any of them. The least popular. Really weird, freaky stuff, the sort that scream "Lock me up." Like, say, scratching off scabs, not wearing underpants on Mondays, Wednesdays and Fridays, pulling my hair out, being scared of puking, committing suicide, killing somebody.

An' I'm not sure, perhaps over the last five years, no, probably less, anyway what the fuck, over the past few years, it's really not been that bad, I mean I do manage to put the brake on, to act sensibly. No new quirk has come my way for going on ten years. Except for one.

I never bring girls back to sleep *chez moi*. I always ask if I can go *chez elles*. I really like seeing where the girl I'm about to bed lives, it intrigues me, even doubles my pleasure.

My belly feels ready to thrust, I get the hots, I get stressed out.

Fact is I lay loads of girls, never do a repeat perf, an' when I leave the morning after, I steal something, I bring back an item from *chez elle* to *chez moi*. An' get freaked out and frantic, am morose for days when I don't, so now I always do. I've got a really great collection of peculiar, rag-bag stuff that looks nothing like, that seems totally random. Only yours truly knows the BIG link.

Last night. I went to the Ninkasi. I met a girl. Mind-blowing. Wonderful. But really too hippy. But hippy ain't right, it's bizarre, she's kind of mongrel, like a mix of New Age, Cowboys Fringants and a touch of Anne-Marie Cadieux. I walked into her place an' we stayed in the pitch dark until we fell asleep, as she ain't got no lights. I kid you not, she ain't got no lights. When I requested: "Could you switch on the light per-lease? I want to take out my contacts," she replied "I ain't got none, but I could light a candle if you like..."

For Christ's sake, I opened my eyes this morning and bugger me, she ain't got a fucking single light, a fucking piece of furniture, a fucking knick-knack, a fucking bauble on her bookshelf, not a thing. I tell you, we were lying on a mattress on the floor in her one-bed flat with a carpet all around us, a plastic tray containing underwear and our shoes. An' that was it. A kind of Feng shui on the cheap.

I stole a roll of toilet paper. Just made it. A last-minute thing.

You know, I'd not stolen anything, we'd only left her place two minutes an' I was stressing real bad, I kept telling myself I'd not sleep for a fortnight, so sod it, I asked if I could go back, I told her I just had to have a piss, that I was like that in the morning, I really needed to piss, or I'd piss my pants, it was some kind of kidney complaint. She said: "I'll wait here," then handed me her keys. I didn't really go for a piss. I stole a roll of toilet paper.

Chez moi in the top of the beige set of drawers in my bedroom I've got:

> a pink and mauve Timex watch that's broke
> a Princess Leia figurine
> a bag of ramen

a sea-blue, yellow-spotted thong
a pocket bible
a volcanic pebble
a DVD remote
a glass for tea
a pair of Dolce & Gabbana specs
a pink lighter with a light underneath
a black, poodle-shaped salt cellar
a can of hot dogs
a cat toy
a small bronze bell
a fluorescent green sock
a wooden beermat
red lipstick
plus a wonderful roll of ass-hole paper
An' funniest of all, that item says everything
there is to say about the night we spent together.

Racily translated by Peter Bush

ABOUT THE TRANSLATOR
Peter Bush is currently working on a volume of
Barcelona Tales for Oxford University Press. His
recent translations from French include Alain
Badiou's *In Praise of Love* and a Maël Renouard
story, 'The Ruins of the Führermuseum.'

THE TRANSLATOR'S APPROACH
"I tried to capture the off-beat, zany tone, and racy rush of words that undercut the basic male bumptiousness, and worried about my lack of familiarity with Quebec French—apart from Michel Tremblay!"

36. Floorboards

LAST NIGHT, I met a choreographer. And I want to make love to her.

I want to put her breasts in my mouth. Because they're the most beautiful breasts I've ever seen in my life.

They're magnificent.

And I want them in my mouth. And in my hands.

Last night, I met a choreographer and I want to make love to her.

I want her to move right in front of me, I want her to move before my eyes because she moves with her hips and it makes me want to make love to her.

Because she moves as if she was on stage, but she talks to you as if she was not on stage, as if she was there for real and she was just talking to you; she's there for real and she just talks to you but she moves unconsciously, as if she was on stage.

She breathes with her back when she walks.

You see it coming
you see her breath rising when she walks
you see that it comes from her back
from her hips
that it rises up to her breasts and that it ends
that it stops
that it goes out
through her mouth, which she brings forward ever so slightly.

Everybody breathes and I never gave a shit about it before
but
last night
I met a choreographer and I noticed that she breathed.

I thought: "Fuck she breathes so beautifully!"

I think it's because she breathes from every-where, she breathes "inside of" everywhere
inside of her fingers
inside of her legs
and inside of her face which is always moving a little.

Last night, I met a choreographer and I want to make love to her because she breathes from everywhere and I thought someone, at some point, should check her pulse, to see how things change in her body, from everywhere, when her heart rate increases.

And it wouldn't bother me at all
I'd definitely volunteer to try the experience and make her heart beat faster
to see

how it reacts over there, how it reacts in her hair, in her hips, in her fingers.

Last night, I met a choreographer and I want to make love to her.

I want her to want to make love to me right now.
I want her to suggest it.

I'd pretend to think about it.

And while I'd be pretending to think about it, she'd think about the things she'd do to me, she'd make a plan of all the things we'd do.

No.

I don't want us to plan anything

I want us to improvise everything

I want us to put our mouths
our hands
our junk
on the table.

I want us to improvise
to let ourselves go.

I want to let myself go, I want the beautiful
choreographer I met last night to consent to me
letting myself go, I want her to tell me that it's
okay, that she's taking care of everything.

I want the beautiful choreographer to
choreograph a night with her, for me.

I want her to start by showing me
I want her to explain by showing me, first.

I want her to stand up and to move
to start on her own while I watch.

And once I have understood
once I have seen
I'll stand up too and we'll do it together.

We'll dance together.

I'll mimic her movements, I'll do the moves
she invented, we'll move together
slowly

so we can take our time putting our hands in
the right places
   putting our breaths in the right places
   putting our rhythms in the right places.

I want her to show me how to breathe prop-
erly, to show me how to breathe from the stomach if she wants, as long as she puts her hands
on my belly.

I want us to put on some music.

I want us to find the perfect lighting, so it
perfectly outlines her perfect little choreographer body.

I want us to go on tour together.

To check in to every hotel room in the world,
to stop by every restaurant bathroom
   to make love on the go.

To go on tour and to take a train across
Europe, in every cab of every European train.
   I want us to sign autographs for everyone.
Nobody will know why we're signing autographs

but we'll sign all the bed sheets anyways, all the tablecloths, all the sidewalks.

I want us to set fire to all the bed sheets, to all the tablecloths, and to all the sidewalks because we're coming by and because that's what we do: set fire to our bellies.

I want us to have fire all over our hands and I want us to set everything on fire so we feel it burn but it doesn't hurt anyone.

I want people to look at us as we set things on fire
barefoot
or wearing a black leotard if she wants people to look at us as we set things on fire rubbing our feet on all the possible floorboards
on all the possible black spaces.

I want us to rub our feet on the floorboards.

I want us to move until fire sparks and we burn
the choreographer that I met last night, her mouth against mine
we burn naked

sitting on the floorboards burning,
our backs to the audience
to a Cinematic Orchestra or a Cat Power song.

I want us to stand up
to be done burning
to grab something to eat and to start burning
again
somewhere else
on other floorboards.

I want all of the world's choreographers to be
jealous of our choreographies.

I want Dave St-Pierre to be jealous of our
choreographies
because ours are even more beautiful than
his.

Because we are even more naked.

Because our floorboards are even wetter.

Approximately translated by Pierre-Luc Landry

ABOUT THE TRANSLATOR
Pierre-Luc Landry is not a translator; he was not trained or schooled as such. He is a writer, an editor, a professor, a polyglot. But at times, when very tired, he can't English anymore. He is a faculty member at the Royal Military College of Canada's French Studies department. *Listening for Jupiter*, Landry's second novel, was recently published by QC Fiction.

THE TRANSLATOR'S APPROACH
"I hesitated a lot. I wanted to be as faithful as possible to the original but I struggle a lot with fidelity so yeah, I wandered, I deviated, I veered, hoping I would be able to convey, in English, all of the poetry and the power of the French story. Appropriating the text was key in consenting, in the end, to only "dire quasi la stessa cosa," as Umberto Eco phrased it. I was not rewriting; I was translating. I learned in the process what that really means."

37. Vinyl

I HAVE A COLLECTION of twenty-four hundred CDs. Before, when I was younger, I used to collect vinyl, like my dad, but I sold everything at 18 when I left for France after the '95 referendum. That night, I was at home, with my family, in Saint-Tite. It was fall, it wasn't nice out, I don't remember much, except that it's the only time in my life that I've seen my dad cry. I don't remember anything except posters with daisies, planets, and peace signs on them; I remember Dédé Fortin crying, my dad crying; I remember, *je me souviens*, that deep down I believed in it, but then later, I stopped believing. The wind was blowing, that I remember, blowing hard, all night. When the wind blows that hard I always feel like it's a kind of personal message directed at me, like a secret code between me and life, to let me know that things are changing, and if they don't change, something's not right.

The next morning I went back to empty out my apartment in Montreal, a four-hour bus ride. I sold all my records, I bought a plane ticket to Paris. I puked on the flight, I think out of grief, helplessness, and hope. Can you puke out of hope? Anyway. It wasn't just about the referendum, or about my dad crying. It was like a kind of heartache, a breakup with the world. Or with myself, I don't really know. I got to France in November, it was never nice out, I started spending my life in the museums. When does it happen? At what point does it slip through our fingers? I don't know. Me, I wanted to draw, be great, have purpose, live in a *chambre de bonne*, eat artichokes and figs and *nouilles au beurre*, smoke Philip Morrises. I was staying at the corner of Saint-Gilles and Turenne, in the Marais, with a girl called Anne-Claire. I was going out with her brother who was married. I met him at the Rodin museum, in front of the Kiss; his nose started bleeding when he saw me, and we both took it as a sign, but we shouldn't have. I stayed in France for four months. And then I ran out of money. I went home. That's it.

Why am I talking about this? Because I could have. Because I believed in it, but then later, I stopped believing. There's always a moment, in everything, love stories, movies, novels, lives, when it's there, it's just a small opening and you need to give everything you've got to get in there, you need to run up and throw yourself, but at the right time and place and at the right person. Because otherwise you get thrown back, and then you just get back on your plane and puke again. I don't get travel sickness. I just missed my shot. And I know it. It wasn't the guy who had a nose-bleed when he first saw me, it wasn't Paris, and it definitely wasn't art. I don't know what happened. Or when it happened. But I passed myself by. I missed myself. If you talk to the people around me, they'll tell you. I think I'm pretty. I have a great job that I don't really feel like talking about. I have a boyfriend who didn't get a nosebleed when he first saw me but who had the exceptional quality of not already being married. We'll probably have a baby soon. Everyone thinks I have a great life. But I don't draw anymore. I don't vote anymore either. My dad died last summer and we had never talked about the referendum or about how upset he was or about his records. They're still in Saint-Tite. Now I have a collection of twenty-four hundred CDs and I never listen to them. I just know that there was a time in my life when I believed in it, when I said this is it, I'm going to have an amazing life, but in the end it wasn't nice out, the guy was married, I was broke, and it didn't happen. I don't know why.

I regret everything about me. If I told anyone, they wouldn't want to believe me.

Every time the wind blows, I wonder if there's a way out. Every time, I don't know what to throw myself at. In whose way. Every time I see a guy, I hope his nose starts bleeding. But it never does.

Fervently translated by Natalia Hero

ABOUT THE TRANSLATOR

Natalia Hero is a writer and translator from Montreal, Canada. Her short fiction has appeared in various online literary magazines such as *Peach Magazine* and *Shabby Doll House*. She is currently pursuing an MA in literary translation at the University of Ottawa.

THE TRANSLATOR'S APPROACH

"It was important to me that none of the cultural specificity of this story be lost in translation. The referendum plays such an important role as the backdrop for this character's emotional crisis that I wanted to make sure that that presence came through in my version. For example, there's a repetition of "je me souviens" in the opening paragraph that I wanted to keep, and that would be lost in English if I just translated it directly, so I quoted it directly in French. My other big concern was register—the original French text reads so fluidly, exactly the way someone from Montreal would speak, and I think that plays a really important role in the story. It really works with this character who's so lost that she tends to ramble. I think there's always a risk when trying to recreate that orality in writing, because sometimes it can come off a little forced, or not realistic. So when I was translating, I read it aloud to myself a few times to make sure it sounded fluid."

About the Translators

Anissa Bachan specializes in French-to-English translation. In 2014 she was hosted by the Banff International Literary Translation Centre. She is also the recipient of a Joseph Armand Bombardier Canada Graduate Scholarship (SSHRC) for her graduate research on the ideological dimensions of political translation in contemporary Quebec.

Melissa Bull, a writer and translator from Montreal, has published fiction, non-fiction, poetry, and translations in a variety of publications. She is the editor of *Maisonneuve* magazine's "Writing from Quebec" column and the author of a book of poetry titled *Rue*. Her translation of Nelly Arcan's *Burqa of Skin* was published in 2014. Melissa currently lives in England.

Peter Bush is currently working on a volume of *Barcelona Tales* for Oxford University Press. His recent translations from French include Alain Badiou's *In Praise of Love* and a Maël Renouard story, 'The Ruins of the Führermuseum.'

Lisa Carter is an acclaimed Spanish-to-English translator whose work has won the Alicia Gordon Award for Word Artistry in Translation and been nominated for the International DUBLIN Literary Award. Through her company, Intralingo Inc., Lisa helps authors and translators bring their works to a whole new audience.

Allison M. Charette founded the Emerging Literary Translators' Network in America. She has received a PEN/Heim Translation Fund Grant and been nominated for the Best of the Net. Her translation of Naivo's *Beyond the Rice Fields*, the first novel from Madagascar to appear in English, is available from Restless Books.

American-born translator **Kathryn Gabinet-Kroo** has been a professional artist for almost 40 years, exhibiting her paintings in Canada and the U.S. Since completing her Master's in Translation Studies at Concordia University, she has been passionate about literary translation. Four of her translated novels have been published by Exile Editions, and excerpts have appeared in the Exile Quarterly and on the Ambos and Québec Reads websites.

Farrah Gillani studied French at school in England, but has managed to avoid it ever since! She is, however, passionate about literature, studying English at Cambridge University and now running an online magazine in Luxembourg. In between, she worked in marketing for Mars, where she was paid in both chocolate and money.

Daniel Grenier was born in Brossard in 1980. In 2012, he published his first collection of short stories, *Malgré tout on rit à Saint-Henri* (Le Quartanier). As of today, he has translated six books for different Quebec publishers like Marchand de feuilles, Boréal, and La Peuplade. In 2014, he completed a doctoral dissertation about the novelist character in American fiction from 1850 to 2007. His first novel, *L'année la plus longue* (Le Quartanier), was published in English by House of Anansi Press in March 2017.

Benjamin Hedley's childhood as a military brat exposed him to life in various places, from British Columbia to Quebec and Germany. An intense interest in literature and culture, as well as a trilingual upbringing have driven him to pursue a difficult yet gratifying career as a literary translator.

Natalia Hero is a writer and translator from Montreal, Canada. Her short fiction has appeared in various online literary magazines such as *Peach Magazine* and *Shabby Doll House*. She is currently pursuing an MA in literary translation at the University of Ottawa.

Cassidy Hildebrand is a freelance translator who studied translation at the University of Ottawa. She loves, in no particular order, music, movies, food, fashion, sports, travelling, reading, writing and translating. She mostly translates jargony, technical stuff, but every now and then, she's lucky enough to translate short stories.

Aleshia Jensen grew up in Winnipeg, Vancouver, and a few places in between. She moved to Montreal in 2007 to study translation, and now freelances from her St. Henri apartment. Her first book-length translation is forthcoming from QC Fiction in 2018.

Pierre-Luc Landry is not a translator; he was not trained or schooled as such. He is a writer, an editor, a professor, a polyglot. But at times, when very tired, he can't English anymore. He is a faculty member at the Royal Military College of Canada's French Studies department. *Listening for Jupiter*, Landry's second novel, was recently published by QC Fiction.

G. Lefebvre is from Shania Twain country. He writes and translates in Quebec City.

Tony Malone is an Anglo-Australian literary reviewer. His site, *Tony's Reading List*, has developed a strong focus on literary fiction in translation, featuring around one hundred reviews of translated literature every year. His reviews have also appeared at

Words Without Borders and *Asymptote*. This is his first attempt at literary translation.

Anna Matthews is a writer and translator based in Minneapolis. She holds an MA in Literary Translation Studies from the University of Rochester. Her creative areas of interest include translating literature from Quebec, particularly women's voices, and writing genre-free prose.

Riteba McCallum lives in Montreal and works as a freelance translator.

Originally from Ireland, **Peter McCambridge** holds a BA in modern languages from Cambridge University, England, and has lived in Quebec City since 2003. He runs Québec Reads and now QC Fiction, a new imprint of Quebec fiction in translation. He has translated seven novels, all from Quebec, and edited this book.

Originally from Romania, **Felicia Mihali** is a journalist, a novelist, and a teacher. She has studied French, English, Chinese, and Dutch, and has specialized in postcolonial literature and history. She now writes in French and in English.

Jessica Moore is an author and translator. *Mend the Living*, Jessica's translation of the moving and unusual story of a heart transplant by French author

Maylis de Kerangal, was nominated for the 2016 Man Booker International Prize. www.jessicamoore.ca

Tom Moore was born in Belfast in 1941 and educated at Royal Belfast Academical Institution and Dublin University. He pursued a career teaching languages in Coleraine, Limavady, and Antrim, Northern Ireland. He's been married since 1969 to Ann, with four sons, the fathers of fifteen grandchildren. He is currently Chair of Examiners for A/AS French at the Council for Curriculum, Examinations, and Assessment and active in the Association of Baptist Churches in Ireland.

Guillaume Morissette is the author of *New Tab* (Véhicule Press, 2014), which was a finalist for the 2015 Amazon.ca First Novel Award. His work has appeared in *Maisonneuve Magazine, Little Brother Magazine, Vice, Electric Literature, The Quietus*, and many other publications. He lives in Montreal.

Rhonda Mullins is a writer and translator living in Montreal. She won the 2015 Governor General's Literary Award for Translation for Jocelyne Saucier's *Twenty-One Cardinals. And the Birds Rained Down*, her translation of Saucier's *Il pleuvait des oiseaux*, was a CBC Canada Reads Selection for 2015. She is also a four-time finalist for the Governor General's Literary Award in Translation.

A writer and certified translator, **Jean-Paul Murray** is secretary of the Gatineau Park Protection Committee. The former managing editor and English translation coordinator of *Cité libre*, he has translated fifteen books, including novels by Robert Lalonde and Louis Hamelin. Ekstasis will publish his translation of Robert Lalonde's *Le monde sur le flanc de la truite* in the coming months.

Dimitri Nasrallah is the author of two award-winning novels, *Niko* (2011) and *Blackbodying* (2005). He is currently translating Eric Plamondon's 1984 trilogy and serves as editor for Véhicule Press's Esplanade Books fiction imprint. His third novel will be published in 2018. He lives in Montreal and teaches at Concordia University.

Marie-Claude Plourde graduated from Université de Montréal in 2004 and is currently working on a Master's thesis at Université Laval on the translation of orality markers in a theatrical corpus. She particularly enjoys texts that pose challenging problems related to the translation of form. She's also fond of Peirce's semiotics.

Lori Saint-Martin is a professor in the Département d'études littéraires, Université du Québec à Montréal. With Paul Gagné, she has translated over 90 books from English to French, winning 3 Governor General's Awards and 4 QWF Translation Prizes.

She also translates from Spanish to French and self-translates from French to English. She enjoys moving between two native languages, one of which she learned in her late teens. She is the author of four works of fiction, including a novel, *Les portes closes,* incomparably translated by the one and only Peter McCambridge.

Ros Schwartz is an award-winning literary translator from French. Since 1979, she has translated over 70 works of Francophone fiction and non-fiction including a new translation of *The Little Prince* by Antoine de Saint-Exupéry and nine works by Georges Simenon. Other authors include Tahar ben Jelloun, Dominique Eddé, Aziz Chouaki, and Dominique Manotti, whose *Lorraine Connection* won a Silver Dagger Award. Founder and co-director of the literary translation summer school at City University in London, Ros frequently leads workshops, is a regular speaker on the international circuit, and publishes articles on translation issues.

Jacob Siefring is a Canadian-American translator. His published translations include *The Major Refutation* by Pierre Senges and Stéphane Mallarmé's long typographical poem *A Roll of the Dice Will Never Abolish Chance*.

Neil Smith wrote the novel *Boo* (Hugh MacLennan Prize) and the story collection *Bang Crunch* (QWF First Book Prize). His fiction has been translated into eight languages. He was a finalist for a Governor General's Award for *The Goddess of Fireflies*, his translation of Geneviève Pettersen's debut novel.

Pablo Strauss grew up in British Columbia and lives in Quebec City. He has translated books by Daniel Grenier (*The Longest Year*) and Maxime Raymond Bock (*Baloney, Atavisms*), and short works by a variety of Quebec authors.

J.C. Sutcliffe is a writer and translator. She has lived in England, France, and Germany, and currently lives in Canada. Her translation of *Document 1* by François Blais will be published by BookThug in 2018.

Translation, navigating words and their multiple meanings, has been part of life for **Michèle Thibeau** since she moved to Quebec City in the early 1990s. Michèle had an opportunity to practice French-to-English translation while at the *Quebec Chronicle-Telegraph*. She continues to dabble, in addition to writing poems and short stories.

Carly Rosalie Vandergriendt is a Montreal-based writer, editor, and translator. Her writing has appeared in *The Malahat Review, Room, Matrix, Plenitude, Cosmonauts Avenue, Riddle Fence*, and elsewhere. She recently completed an MFA in Creative Writing through UBC's optional-residency program. Visit her at www.carlyrosalie.com or follow her on Twitter @carlyrosalie.

David Warriner emerged largely unscathed from an Oxford education and narrowly escaped the graduate rat race by hopping on a plane to Quebec. Fifteen years into a premium commercial translation career, he listened to his heart and decided to turn his hand again to the delicate art of literary translation.

Elizabeth West is a French-to-English translator and editor based in Quebec City. Her early love affair with words, leading to bachelor's degrees in French and English literature and translation from the Universities of Toronto and Ottawa, has resulted in this first foray into literary translation.

Emily Wilson is a translator and writer mostly based in Montreal, at least when the weather's OK. When she isn't agonizing over the wording of a sentence, she's fighting Muay Thai to the death or just trying to keep her cat off the computer.

About the Authors

Born in Chicoutimi in 1985, **Steve Gagnon** later moved to Quebec City, where he studied drama at the Conservatoire d'art dramatique de Québec. Steve is a talented director and actor, appearing on television and the stage in the likes of *Romeo and Juliet*, *Caligula*, and *The Odyssey*, among many other productions. His play *La montagne rouge (SANG)* was a finalist for the 2011 Governor General's award, and he has written a number of others (*Ventre*, *En dessous de vos corps, je trouverai ce qui est immense et qui ne s'arrête pas*, and *Fendre les lacs*) as well as this collection of monologues (*Chaque automne j'ai envie de mourir*), which he co-wrote with Véronique Côté, and an essay on life as a man in the 21st century (*Je serai un territoire fier et tu déposeras tes meubles*). He co-founded the theatre company Jésus, Shakespeare et Caroline and now lives in Montreal.

Véronique Côté was born in Quebec City in 1980 and works as an actress, author, and director, often focusing on the beauty of everyday life. She has performed in close to thirty productions since graduating from the Conservatoire d'art dramatique de Québec in 2002, most notably in Wajdi Mouawad's critically acclaimed *Forêts*, in Quebec and France. *Tout ce qui tombe*, her first text for the theatre, was a finalist for the Governor General's award in 2013, and she has since co-written *Attentat*, *S'appartenir(e)*, and *La fête sauvage*. She has published an essay on poetry (*La vie habitable*) as well as this collection (*Chaque automne j'ai envie de mourir*), which she co-wrote with Steve Gagnon. Véronique lives in Quebec City, but spends much of her time in Montreal.

Praise for previous QC Fiction titles

"Wildly imaginative [...] a remarkably sensitive and intelligent coming-of-age story told with an irresistible blend of heartache, humour, and magic."

(Joseph Schreiber, *Numéro Cinq*, on *Life in the Court of Matane*)

■

"This debut novel is highly original, shifting between levity and darkness with a masterful hand."

(Rhonda Mullins, *The Malahat Review*, on *The Unknown Huntsman*)

■

"The prose can be as ominous and as vivid as Cormac McCarthy's *Child of God*. It is testament to Katia Grubisic's translation that such an analogy is not hyperbolic. [...] This is an extraordinary first novel by an enormously talented writer, and a first translation by an enormously talented poet-translator."

(Des Barry, *3:AM Magazine*, on *Brothers*)

Printed in July 2017
by Gauvin Press,
Gatineau, Québec